# PROTECTING REBEL

## Katie Reus

KR Press, LLC

Cover art by Sweet 'N Spicy Designs
Editor: Kelli Collins
Proofreader: Book Nook Nuts
Author website: https://www.katiereus.com

Publisher's Note: This is a work of fiction. Names, characters, places, and incidents are either the products of the author's imagination or used fictitiously, and any resemblance to actual persons, living or dead, or business establishments, organizations or locales is completely coincidental.

Protecting Rebel /Katie Reus. -- 1st ed.

# DEDICATION

*For Kaylea Cross, who is about to jump into a new adventure.*

# PROLOGUE

*Thirteen years ago*

Rebel's heart rate kicked into high gear as Weston pulled up his bedroom window for her. "You don't need to sneak in the window, you can just go to the front door," he said even as he stood back and let her crawl into his room. Sometime in the last year he'd bulked up, filled out, and *ohmygod* he was gorgeous. They'd been friends since they were twelve and she'd always had a little crush on him, but since she'd turned seventeen, the way she felt now was different.

"I know, but my mom's boyfriend is in the driveway. He just pulled up. He's earlier than I thought so I climbed out my window to avoid seeing him at all." She'd been avoiding him for two months to perfection. And as soon as she graduated, she was moving out, even if she wasn't sure where she was going to live.

Weston looked as if he wanted to murder the guy, but she shook her head. "He hasn't touched me or anything. It's just... whatever. My mom's passed out and I just didn't want to be there, that's all." Lies of course. Well, the guy hadn't touched her exactly, but the way he looked at her was enough to make her want to puke. She fought off a shudder. Gross.

He was around forty and smelled like whisky all the time. And what kind of forty-year-old looked at a seventeen-year-old the way he looked at her? Ugh. "You think Aunt Margaret will care if I stay tonight?" Because her mom was supposed to go into work later and she wouldn't care if her boyfriend stayed while she was gone.

Her mom didn't care about anyone but herself. And getting high, of course.

They were going to lose the house soon, something she wasn't even sure if her mom realized. Or more likely she was just living in her permanent state of denial. But the foreclosure notices and past due property taxes had started arriving over the last couple months so she had to know. Rebel wasn't even angry anymore, just disappointed. Her mom lived completely detached from reality most days, but she still held down a job. Rebel was pretty sure she was drinking or snorting her money away, however. It was the only thing that made sense.

"Of course you can stay." He frowned as if her question was ludicrous, but she never wanted to be a burden. His aunt—who insisted that Rebel call her aunt too—was so kind and giving and Rebel never wanted to take advantage. But she felt safe here. Safer than anywhere else.

"Is your aunt home yet? If not I'll make dinner."

"Rebel." Weston sat on the edge of his bed, his expression serious. "You don't have to cook or whatever to hang out here."

"I know," she whispered, sitting next to him. She laid her head on his shoulder, the only time she ever felt truly safe. With him. And she knew he'd be leaving soon. He hadn't actually said the words but she'd seen the paperwork he'd tried to hide from her. "I don't want to feel like a burden," she whispered, her greatest fear. Well, one of them.

She was also terrified of failing, of not taking her shot. Of having a bunch of regrets and ending up an addict like her mom.

"Shut up with that shit," Weston muttered in that gruff way of his. "A burden." He snorted as if the idea was ridiculous, making her smile as he nudged her gently with his shoulder.

Somehow he always knew what to say. "I can't believe we graduate in a month," she murmured, wanting to change the subject.

She'd been writing songs and posting videos of herself online singing a lot over the last year. And recently she'd been contacted by a couple different agents and wasn't sure what to do. But she didn't want to let fear hold her back. She'd promised Aunt Margaret that she'd finish high school before she made any decisions about where to move. Because she wasn't going to college, that much she was sure of. She had no desire to and it was too expensive anyway. What would the point be for someone like her? To get a bunch of debt and a degree that meant nothing? No thanks. All she wanted to do was sing and perform, and she didn't need a degree for it.

"I know." Leaning forward on the bed, he scrubbed his hands over his face.

"Are you ever going to tell me about the Marines?" she asked quietly.

He stilled, then looked back at her before he shifted on the bed, faced her completely. "You know about that?"

"Of course I know. You're my best friend." She took his hands in hers, squeezed tight. God, he was the best friend she'd ever had. When she was younger, she'd wished he was her brother. But then... a few years ago, her feelings had most decidedly shifted and nothing she felt for him was sisterly. Not even close. And when he stared at her now with those blue eyes that made her think of the Caribbean—not that she'd ever been—she knew she could easily get lost in them. "Plus I saw some paperwork from a recruiter the other day."

He was completely still as he watched her and not for the first time, she thought how unnerving it was to be on the end of that intense stare. But not in a bad way. And she always wondered what it would be like if he was solely focused on her in very different circumstances. But he only looked at her like a friend, that much she was sure of.

"So what do you think?"

"I'm happy for you." From the time they were twelve it was all he'd talked about. His dad had died overseas while in the Marine Corps when Weston was eleven, and that was when he'd come to live with Aunt Margaret—the woman he'd been named after, Margaret Weston.

And he'd changed Rebel's life forever.

He'd been crying the first time she'd seen him in Aunt Margaret's backyard and had tried to hide it. But she'd hugged him and that had been that. Instant best friends.

He'd always wanted to follow in his dad's footsteps and she knew that once he put his mind to something, he would do it. He was determined like that, something she appreciated.

"Thanks. It's just… scary I guess," he murmured, as if he didn't want to admit it.

"Of course it's scary." She was scared too. Of losing him.

"I don't want to lose contact with you," he blurted.

She blinked, surprised he would ever think that. She smacked his knee. "Lose contact? I'm going to email you every day, dumbass. And if they let you have a phone, I'll text you every day."

He gave her a ghost of a smile, transforming his face completely. Some of the kids at school said he looked scary, and she could see that. But when he smiled… she felt it all the way to her toes. She could make some very bad decisions if he ever decided to smile at her as if he wanted more than friendship. So it was probably good that he never had. He knew her better than anyone, saw the real her. Knew all her dreams and hopes and told her to go for them. Having a friend like him was worth more than anything.

"I don't think I can have a phone while I'm in boot camp, but okay."

"Just *okay*?"

"I mean, *good*," he said, laughing. "So much is changing. I'm just starting to get in my head I guess."

"It's not too late to change your mind." A selfish part of her hoped he might, but then she chastised herself. He'd always supported her and she simply wanted him to be happy, to go for what he wanted.

"No, I don't want to." He got a far-off look on his face, then shook himself. "Come on. Let's go cook dinner before Aunt Margaret gets home. I'm going to tell her tonight."

Rebel had a feeling that his aunt wasn't going to be surprised, but nodded. She'd follow Weston anywhere.

***

"I'm so proud of you." Aunt Margaret pulled Weston into a tight hug. "Though I'll probably try to pack myself away in your duffle bag when it finally becomes real."

Rebel giggled as she picked up their plates from the table.

"Darlin', leave that," Aunt Margaret admonished, waving her hands at Rebel.

But Rebel just ignored her and gathered everything up even as dread filled her stomach. Soon she'd have to go home. Her mom's car was gone and so was her mom's boyfriend's car, but he could come back later. She'd just lock her bedroom door, she told herself. And ignore him if he tried to bother her.

"We're going to go out for ice cream to celebrate. How does that sound? Or do you kids have homework?"

Rebel laughed at the same time Weston did.

"It's the last month of school," he murmured.

"It's like a free-for-all this month," she added. "Especially for us since we're seniors."

Margaret nodded, pleased. "Good. Then we're going for ice cream and then maybe we'll go to that fancy arcade on Brickell."

Rebel lifted a shoulder as she looked at Weston. She really wanted to go, anything to avoid going home, but it was his decision.

"Yeah, that sounds really good," he said, grinning.

The 'fancy arcade' was a three-story gaming place that had recently opened up and they both loved it. And might have even skipped school a couple times to hang out there with some friends from the neighborhood.

"Also, there's something I wanted to talk to you about, Rebel." Margaret was suddenly serious, motioning for Rebel to sit back down at the kitchen table. "I'd like you to move in here. No pressure, but we've got that extra room and..." She sighed. "Your mom's house is no good for you now. You're about to graduate and I think you should just move in now and—"

"Yes!" She blurted the word out before she could stop herself. Deep down she worried that Margaret was doing this out of pity, but the fear of going home outweighed any of it. And god knew, her mom wouldn't care or even notice. That place wasn't a real home anyway, not like here with people who cared about her.

"I'm not going to tell my mom," she whispered. "If that's okay?'

Margaret just shrugged. "You're almost eighteen and truthfully, I don't think she'll notice, hon."

Sadly it was true. A hint of pain settled in her chest, but she was starting to accept that her mom was who she was. Nothing would change someone that selfish. "She works late, so can I bring over my stuff tonight?" She worried that it was too soon, but both Weston and his aunt nodded immediately.

"We'll grab whatever you need before heading out." Margaret grinned at her as she said it. "And I just want you to know that I hope you take your shot with singing. If you have to take crappy, low-paying jobs, I don't want you to worry about having to pay rent or anything. You can live here as long as you want and don't have to worry about any bills other than what you already pay for yourself. I just... you've got so much talent and I want you to focus on your music. I have no idea what all of that entails but—"

Rebel threw her arms around the petite older woman. "Thank you," she whispered around the tears. Margaret was the only person aside from Weston who had ever supported her dreams. It meant the world to her.

"Oh, hon." Margaret patted her back gently. "You're one of my own and family looks out for family."

Her throat tightened and she had to push back the tears before she embarrassed herself. This was a gift she couldn't turn down. And she swore that one day when she was finally making real money, she was going to pay Aunt Margaret back a hundred fold.

Hours later, when it was well after midnight, Rebel stared up at the ceiling of the little guest room, feeling more at peace than she could ever remember.

Completely safe.

It was a strange feeling, to be... secure. Not to worry about whether or not she would have a roof over her head next month. Not to worry about her mom busting the door open drunk in the middle of the night and demanding to know where Rebel had hidden her vodka. *Spoiler alert*, she'd never hidden it. Her mom had just always drunk it, then forgot about it.

It was even better not having to worry about one of her mom's pervert boyfriends trying to get into her room late at night.

As she lay there, savoring this new sensation, something made her sit up. A sound. Frowning, she slid out of bed and stepped into the hallway.

And saw Weston stepping out of his bedroom fully dressed and disheveled. "Weston?"

"It's fine, just go back to bed."

Yeah, so that wasn't happening. They'd gotten in an hour ago after the best night out and they'd all gone to bed, so what was he doing? Frowning, she followed after him and realized his knuckles were bloody. "Oh my god," she whispered, shutting the bathroom door behind them. His aunt had a bathroom to herself but there was only one other one and it was cramped. Especially with how big Weston had gotten recently. "What happened?" she demanded even as she opened the bottom cabinet and pulled out the first-aid kit.

"Nothing." He shoved his dark hair off his forehead and avoided looking at her as she started cleansing his right hand. The worst of the two.

"This doesn't look like nothing." Only three of the four lightbulbs worked in the bathroom and she made a mental note to change the blown one as she said, "Look, if I'm going to be your alibi, then I need to know what I'm covering for."

He laughed lightly, but it was short lived. "I just took care of something, that's all. It's not important."

After cleaning the blood off, she started dabbing ointment on each knuckle. "Are you hurt anywhere else?"

"No and I'm fine, I swear. The other guy is a hell of a lot worse, believe me." And he sounded smug about that.

She snapped her gaze up to his. "Weston... did you go next door?"

He stared right at her but didn't respond.

"Weston."

"I don't want to lie to you."

"Then don't lie."

"Fine, I beat the shit out of your mom's boyfriend, okay? He doesn't know it was me. I wore a mask and made sure he knew that he needed to get the hell out of this neighborhood. I'm leaving soon and I won't be able to look out for you! I *had* to do it." Desperation laced his words as he looked down at her imploringly, but also defiantly. As if he wasn't sorry at all. And she didn't think he had any guilt.

Ohhh. Her heart ached at the fear on his face and worry in his voice. God, she was lucky to have him in her life. Setting the ointment down, she wrapped her arms around him. "I want to tell you that violence is the wrong answer but..." She trailed off, tried not to think about the way her mom's boyfriend had 'casually' and not so accidentally rubbed up against her multiple times. Or the times she'd heard her bedroom door handle rattling until her mom's voice called out, looking for him.

"Not always." His grip tightened. "Sometimes violence is the only thing that works."

She leaned into him, into this moment, and wished she could freeze it in time. Things were going to change in a month. They'd both be going in different directions, carving out a place in the world.

But the one thing she knew, she was never ever letting him out of her life. Even if he'd be taking a part of her heart when he left. He could keep it though. And maybe one day... maybe he'd see her as more than a friend.

# CHAPTER 1



*Present day*

Rebel glanced around the interior road of the cemetery as she parked behind a blue truck. She'd had to be sneaky heading here before the funeral procession arrived. The last thing she wanted was for the attention to be taken away from Margaret Weston's funeral and put on her.

And unfortunately because of who she was—a rising musical star—Rebel knew it was a reality. So she'd snuck in the back of the funeral service at the nondenominational church wearing a blonde wig and a plain black dress. No one had given her a second look and as she'd left the church after, she hadn't seen any paparazzi.

Of course, her agent had dropped a few hints online that she was headed up to Fort Lauderdale for the day for some boating thing. Lies that had hopefully helped give her some anonymity for the day.

Even so, she was still debating whether she should even reach out to Weston and tell him that she was here. Phone in her hand, she stared at the black screen in indecision and—

A knock on the driver's side door made her jump. When she saw the man himself standing on the other side wearing a dark suit and an unreadable expression, she winced. He probably didn't realize it was her and was going to ask her to move her car. This area was reserved for the burial.

"Hey," she said after rolling down the window. "It's me. I—"

"I know it's you. Saw you hurry out of the church," he growled, tugging the door open. Then he surprised her by pulling her into a giant hug.

Tears stung her eyes as she wrapped her arms around him and buried her face against his chest. "I'm so sorry about Aunt Margaret." She'd been keeping it together pretty well, but being in his arms now, she could let herself grieve. They'd been friends since they were kids so she tried not to inhale his dark, masculine scent like a perv but it was hard not to when he was a solid eleven inches taller than her and she had her face buried against him.

"Thank you. And thank you for coming. You should have been sitting up at the front with me." His mouth was tight as he pulled back to look down at her.

Just like always, getting an eyeful of him took her breath away. Even now, at the most inappropriate time ever. But she was only human and he was built like a god. Though she knew he worked hard for his body, running something like ten miles every morning with the kind of discipline she appreciated.

"I wasn't sure if you wanted me..." She trailed off at the admonishing look he gave her. She threw up her hands. "You know what I mean," she murmured, glancing around at the cars arriving. Most parked in a line, one behind the other, people getting out and making their way to the burial site. There'd been a lot of people in the church. About five hundred, so it had been easy enough to blend in at the back, but there seemed to be a lot less here. Maybe by Weston's request. "I didn't want to take away focus on her."

"You're family. You'll be sitting with me now." There was a tight set to his jaw, his ice-blue eyes flashing, as if he expected her to argue.

Obviously she wasn't going to. "Of course. I know this is a dumb question, but how are you doing?"

"Okay. We knew it was coming but... it's still hard."

Rebel nodded, swallowing back a rush of tears and emotions. "Last time I talked to her she looked... Well, she looked ready to be done with this world."

Rebel had used video chat to talk to her a few times a week, even while on tour over the last year. They'd talked eight days ago and Margaret had looked exhausted and simply done with everything.

His mouth curved up the smallest fraction. "Yeah, she told me as much. God, I'm glad you're here."

"I should have—"

"Stop, because I know what you're going to say." He reached into the car and pulled the keys from the ignition. Then he wrapped an arm around her in what felt like a protective move. "I can't tell you how much joy she got from seeing you perform. And she told me all about your phone calls, so you were there for her in the exact way she needed."

"I... okay." She'd flown home to Miami multiple times to see Aunt Margaret over the last year but it didn't feel like enough.

"So when did you go blonde?" Weston was tall, solid and hard-looking. He wasn't classically handsome, not in the way a lot of the men in her business tended to be. He was rougher around the edges and becoming a billionaire hadn't changed that. His frown deepened as he glanced at her.

She slid her sunglasses on as they walked across the grassy area, kept her voice low. "It's just a wig. A really good one."

"Hmm."

"What's that mean?"

"That I'm glad you didn't change your hair."

Oh. She blinked, wasn't sure how to respond. Not that he seemed to need a response.

As they approached the organized chairs, Rebel's stomach tightened when she saw Elliana sitting next to Van, one of Weston's business partners. The woman worked with him and was perfectly nice, but Rebel always felt like the worst version of herself around the stunning woman. Something about the tall blonde with perfect *everything* brought up all her childhood insecurities. Not that the woman had ever done anything unkind to Rebel. If anything, she was always so nice, and in a genuine way.

As she and Weston approached, Rebel put a little space between them. There was only one empty seat left and it was clearly Weston's. "I'll just sit in the back—"

Elliana popped up from her seat and was already shaking her head. "No, you're taking this seat."

"Are you sure?" she asked.

The pretty woman clasped Rebel's hand, her expression sincere. "Of course. I barely knew Margaret but I know how much she thought of you. Please, sit here. You're family."

Throat tight, all Rebel could do was nod and collapse into the black folding chair as tears blurred her eyes. Thankfully her sunglasses hid everything. She wanted to not like this gorgeous woman but Elliana was kind and... ugh. Whatever. This was a funeral of the woman who'd had a big hand in raising Rebel. Right now was about the man she'd been obsessed with for longer than she wanted to think about. She needed to keep it together, not give in to some stupid jealousy that she had no right to feel.

Too bad her head was all over the place.

"I feel bad taking her spot," Rebel murmured to Weston as he sat next to her, aware of more people arriving, the seats behind them filling up.

"Don't." His voice was even as he put an arm around her chair, barely skimming her back.

She'd thought that he and Elliana had something going on, but had never been brave enough to ask. Because she was afraid of the answer. If they were together, then she felt more than weird sitting here with him.

"Aunt Margaret left a few things for you," he said quietly, his voice barely audible over the murmurs of the arriving mourners. "Her vinyls, mostly." His voice was tight and she had to close her eyes to stop the deluge of tears.

"Damn it," she muttered and before she could attempt to blink them away, he handed her a tissue. "Thanks." Of course Margaret had left her vinyls. She was the one who'd given Rebel her very first guitar. She sniffled, dabbing at her eyes under her sunglasses.

She hadn't exactly forgotten how bright it was in Miami, but she'd been traveling for the better part of the year and all her performances were at night. She'd been living like a vampire for the most part, seeing various cities at night.

"Do you think you'd have time tonight to meet up, have dinner?" he whispered.

"Of course." She had a concert tomorrow night; the kick off to the end of her tour in her hometown of Miami. "Do you need help with anything before then?"

"No... Hold on." He stood, hugged an older woman who approached and Rebel took the time to glance around at the arriving mourners.

Margaret had been incredibly loved. The woman had been a teacher for years, then after she'd 'retired' she started volunteering at the local library as well as giving her time mentoring and tutoring. It was like she'd been born with this unending well of energy and light—until the stupid cancer had cut her life too short.

But even then, Margaret had been a fighter until the end.

"I wasn't sure if that was you," the man next to her said.

Rebel turned, frowned at the familiar voice. "Oh shit." Then she winced, realizing how loud that had come out. "Fox?" She leaned over and hugged him—the man who'd once been a scrawny boy in the same neighborhood she'd grown up in. "Sorry, I didn't even realize it was you." But of course it was, because this row appeared to be all people from the old neighborhood. Jesus, she had absolutely no awareness today with grief clouding her head.

He hugged her back tight. "I hate the circumstances but it's good to see you. Auntie always talked about you, even had a picture of you, her and Weston from one of your concerts years ago at the hospital with her."

Okay, that she hadn't known. She grabbed for the tissue again.

Charles Fox, though she'd only ever called him Fox, wrapped an arm around her shoulders, squeezed once. "Didn't mean to make you cry more."

"It's fine. I mean, it's a shitty day. I'll be crying all day."

"You coming to the reception after?"

"Ah... I don't think so." She wouldn't be able to blend in.

He nodded in understanding. "I get it. I take it that's a wig?"

"Yeah."

"It's a good one, but you look better as a brunette."

She snorted softly. "Thanks." That seemed to be the consensus. "I'm back in town for a while after the concert. I'd like to catch up, see everyone from the old neighborhood." She'd already talked to some others, including a friend who owned an animal shelter. She was going to be doing some free marketing for them over the weekend.

"Anytime," he said as Weston sat back down, having talked to a throng of people.

Weston not so gently nudged Fox's arm off the back of Rebel's seat, making her frown.

But then he said to Fox, "Come on." Then, "We'll be back," he murmured to her before stalking off and falling in line with a couple other men, and that was when she realized that he and Fox were pallbearers. Of course they were.

The deepest sense of loneliness swept over her as the two of them, along with four other familiar faces, stood and headed for the casket.

Margaret was really gone. The last person she'd ever considered family; a woman who'd been more of a mother to her than her actual flesh and blood, was gone.

And there was nothing her money or fame could do about it. Because she would have stopped today if she could have.

# CHAPTER 2

*Ten years ago*

Weston,

I hope you get this! Been a few weeks since I heard from you. I'm currently in… omg, I had to think about it. But I'm in North Carolina right now. Wilmington specifically. My agent has me opening for this new, hot all-girl band and the schedule is wild. But I'm learning a lot and getting to write the songs I want. The travel is hard but I've made some friends so there's that. How are you? Your last email was so vague and I understand why. I just hate that I haven't seen you in so long. I miss your face. Are you going to get leave for Christmas? If so let me know. I might be able to get back to Miami. Oh, I text with Aunt Margaret every other day and I think she's dating one of our neighbors but won't give me any details. She's a sneaky one. Anyway, I hope to talk to you soon.

xo,
Rebel

***

Rebel,

Sorry it's been a minute. Haven't had phone or email access for *reasons*. That's great about the tour. I wish I could see you perform. If you have pictures feel free to send them. Or even videos. I always knew you'd make it and I can see the trajectory of your career now. You're going to slay. I'm attaching a picture so you can see the shithole I'm in. I officially hate sand and don't think I'll ever voluntarily go to the beach again. Not sure about Christmas but I don't think so. We're not going anywhere at this point. Oh, the two in the picture with me are Van and Elliana. Next time we get leave they said they're coming to Miami with me so I hope you can come too. You'll love them both. But not more than me. :-) Even if I don't write back right away, you can keep emailing. We've got some entertainment here but not much and I love your letters. I miss you too.

—Weston

# CHAPTER 3

"This place is fantastic," Rebel murmured as Weston pulled out the chair for her. "Did you... like rent out the whole place?"

"Ah, I own it." Which was still hard to get used to—having a ridiculous amount of money. But after being one of the original investors in a security app that had recently taken off—and then blown up into so much more in the last year—his entire world had changed in ways he was still processing. "So sort of."

The Italian restaurant had a limited seating capacity and the two front windows overlooked a quiet street that was only busy during daytime hours. It was in a residential neighborhood, making it fairly unique. The interior was all dark wood seating, dark flooring and mostly brick walls. Other than updating the bar area and adding an inviting outdoor seating area, Weston hadn't changed the rest of the mood of the place.

"That's incredible that you bought this place."

He shrugged. Having the kind of money he did now was a huge adjustment. "I just thought eating here would be easier since it's so close to your hotel." The only reason he brought it up was because he wanted to know if she was staying at the hotel with her "friend" Anthony, as the online rags had said she was. Maybe he wasn't as subtle as he thought but it was hard to care.

"Oh, thank you. I'm not really staying at the hotel though."

"You're not?" It had been all over the gossip rags that she was staying at the five-star hotel right by the concert venue for the weekend with her Anthony—and Weston was embarrassed that he occasionally read the online trash. Usually because Elliana wanted to know when Rebel was in town. The badass weapons expert he worked with was a superfan but too embarrassed to ever admit it to Rebel. And she'd sworn him to secrecy too.

Rebel snorted. "No. Of course not. I'm staying at my *home*. It's one of the reasons we planned the tour to end here. So I could finally get back home. And I can't believe you buy into what you read online anyway."

He simply lifted a shoulder, tried not to stare at her too hard. He was beyond raw today after saying his final goodbye to the woman who'd been a mom to him, had raised him. So being here with the woman of his dreams, the woman he'd been in love with before he even understood what that meant... he was questioning his sanity by inviting Rebel out. "Blame Elliana, not me," he grumbled, feeling only slightly embarrassed.

Rebel blinked at him, her dark eyes full of surprise. She tucked a lock of her thick, dark hair behind her ear. "Oh..." She cleared her throat, her expression shifting to one he couldn't read. "So, I kind of can't believe you bought this place. That's a huge deal," she murmured, glancing around the interior of the small Italian restaurant.

"Yeah, I've been 'diversifying my portfolio,'" he said, using air quotes. He knew that restaurants were risky, but he'd done his research before buying this one.

Which made her snicker, the action lightening the tenseness in her expression. He was glad she hadn't worn that wig again, that he could see all of her. Her hair was dark, thick and normally she pulled it back in a twist or in some sort of updo. But she'd left it down tonight, the waves falling past her breasts. And she'd worn her glasses, which he rarely saw her wearing in online pictures. But the square brown speckled frames made her dark, amber-flecked eyes pop more than usual.

She paused as the sommelier arrived at the table, opened the bottle of wine he'd chosen ahead of time, and let them both taste it before he quietly walked away.

"I used to think I couldn't taste the difference between a cheap glass of wine and the mid-level stuff but this... is gold," she said, smiling widely. God, her smile was magnetic. She pulled people in with her authenticity as much as her talent, and her smile was huge and real. Sometimes it was hard to remember that she was only five foot three because her personality was larger than life. And when she performed... it was goddamn magic.

He grinned in spite of the heaviness in his heart. Because he was sitting here with his Rebel, who wasn't really his at all. But she *was* his lifelong friend, the one who understood him, who had grown up with him. The one who'd written him countless emails while he'd been overseas, had always been the voice of reason when they'd been growing up. One of the few people he would trust with his life. Even when she'd been climbing the charts and making a name for herself, she'd never once eased back on their friendship. If anything, she'd latched on tighter.

"I agree. And I went ahead and told the chef what to cook before we got here. Not in a douchey way, but I figured you didn't want to deal with a lot of people today and I know what you like. So I took a chance."

"If this had been a date, I'd be annoyed, but thank you. The thought of making any more choices right now is too much..." She mock shuddered. "So is it weird to own a restaurant and who knows what else now? And yes, I'm being super nosy because I feel like we haven't truly talked in months."

"A little." He nodded slowly, trying not to think about her on a date with anyone else. And she wasn't wrong. They'd texted but the last six months was the only time in their lives when they hadn't had many phone conversations. Even when he'd been in Afghanistan he'd talked to her more. But his work had been insane and she'd added on more stops for her current tour. "Or maybe a lot." He hadn't made much in the military but he'd banked almost all of it for years, giving him enough of a nest egg to invest in the app when the opportunity had arisen.

But he'd also invested in something else—her. She had no idea that he'd contributed to a marketing campaign and he still hadn't decided if he should tell her.

"But we've been working so hard it's almost impossible to even think about all the changes in my life. The only reason I even have downtime right now is..." He cleared his throat as that darkness threatened to pull him under. Because Aunt Margaret had gotten sick.

Rebel reached her hand across the table, her purple fingernails skimming over his forearm. "I know. God, I miss her."

He placed one hand over hers, glad for the small, intimate table and the fact that there was no one else here other than waitstaff. Out of the corner of his eye, he saw their server step out of the kitchen with plates in his hand, then disappear back into the kitchen. Good. Weston didn't want an interruption now. "Me too. So how long are you in town after the concert?" he asked, trying to stay on a neutral enough topic.

And because he desperately wanted her to be in Miami for as long as possible.

"Ah… for a while I think." She pulled her hand back, her face doing that thing where he couldn't read her. And he hated when she did that, made her expression perfectly neutral. She'd been doing it since they were kids, masking everything for whatever reason. He knew she trusted him, but he also knew that she'd grown up putting on a happy face for her shitty mom.

"I hope I get to see more of you."

"And I hope I get to see your new house," she said around a grin.

He'd told her that he'd bought a new place, but hadn't mentioned that it was in her neighborhood. But when a place had come up for sale in the exclusive gated community, he'd jumped on it. For more reasons than he wanted to admit to himself. "Anytime you want. So how's Anthony?" Weston hoped the question sounded casual enough, but was glad when the server approached with their plates. Because that stupid article had said she was staying with him at the nearby hotel instead of her home. The implications had been crystal clear.

"Oh, he's great." Her eyes brightened when she saw the caprese salads, Bolognese and eggplant parmigiana. Then she glanced around, as if making sure no one could overhear them.

Weston had made sure that wouldn't happen. He knew how much she valued her privacy and how hard it was for her to get it. They had a skeleton staff tonight and no one was supposed to bother her or take pictures. Everyone was getting paid triple to be here as well.

She leaned forward, and he so totally did not flick his gaze to the V of her black sweater. "He's thinking of leaving his label and since I know you won't tell anyone, I have standing permission from him to tell you anything."

Weston blinked. "Seriously?"

"Oh yeah. Anthony *adores* you. He's always asking about you."

Well that was a surprise. Weston could admit that he'd always been standoffish with Rebel's friend/whatever the hell the handsome bastard was to her. They were linked together online *all* the time. Something Elliana loved to grill him about. "Oh, great. I'm glad he's doing well." Weston rolled his eyes at himself. He sounded like a moron.

"I know you said no, but do you need help with anything? Like, I don't know, organizing Margaret's stuff or... anything."

He dug his fork into the Bolognese. "She was, not surprisingly, organized even in death. Or maybe because of it. When she got her diagnosis, she went into manic cleaning mode." He set his fork down as his throat tightened with emotions. "I don't know if she knew this was it or if she was just being her normal organized self. But she handled everything."

"Like always," Rebel murmured, her own eggplant parmigiana barely touched as she took a sip of wine. "Remember the time she caught you sneaking out of your bedroom to go bike riding with me?"

It had been like ten o'clock on a random Wednesday and they'd been maybe twelve. Weston didn't remember why Rebel had wanted to go out, though he was sure it had something to do with not wanting to be under the same roof as her deadbeat mom. And he'd agreed to anything she'd asked of him. Always had. He snorted. "She got on her bike and joined us like nothing was out of the ordinary."

"She had this way of making you feel special. *Seen.*" Rebel blinked rapidly, then cleared her throat. "I thought I was all cried out, sorry."

"Don't apologize." Ever. He glanced over at the kitchen doors, saw a couple faces peeking out of the glass windows of the swinging doors.

"What?" She followed his line of sight but the faces quickly disappeared.

"Ah. You've got some fans. I ordered them to stay scarce but..." He shrugged, pushing down his annoyance.

To his surprise, she just laughed. "Oh my god, you probably terrified your employees."

He started to say they weren't his employees. But they were, even if he didn't manage the day-to-day stuff. "I don't terrify anyone. I politely asked."

His words made her laugh even harder. "Um, okay. It's sad that you actually think that. You're terrifying sometimes. I think it's because you're so tall. And your face is intimidating."

"My *face*?"

She gestured with her hand, her gold bracelets clinking together. "Yeah, you know. Mr. Tough Former Military Guy. You're like a... what are those guys called? Drill sergeants."

"My drill *instructor* was a sadistic bastard. I'm nothing like him." God, he'd dreamed of punching that guy in the face more than once. Now he appreciated him, but back then? Hell no.

"He says with a straight face," she said, still laughing.

And the sound was actual music to his ears. He cracked a grin, something in his chest lightening at the way she relaxed with him. "Fine, I might have scared them a little."

"After we eat this amazing food, let's go to the back and say hi to everyone. I can even take some pictures if you're okay with it. And post them on social media?"

"The woman who runs all my social media accounts is going to be thrilled if you do that." She'd already asked Weston if they could stage some photos with Rebel here—an idea he'd promptly shut down. He'd set up tonight because he'd wanted some privacy with her. He didn't want her to feel that she was on display or had to be "on".

And hell, he'd wanted to show off for her just a little. Which made him uncomfortable to admit even to himself.

"Then we'll do it. And your chef is incredible," she said, finally taking a full bite now that the cloud of grief had eased a little.

Aaaand, the slight moan she made went straight to his dick.

Oh hell. He was in serious trouble where she was concerned. Something he'd been aware of for a long damn time. But whenever she was in the same orbit as him, his entire world fell off its axis and he felt out of control.

***

Weston hung back as Rebel worked her magic on the staff. The previous owner had been about to shut down after years of making poor business choices when Weston had swooped in, bought the place and made some changes, including a full staff turnover. Now the place was thriving and the servers his new manager had recently hired were all locals in the neighborhood and currently staring at Rebel as if she was an angel.

Which wasn't too far from the truth.

She was so far out of his stratosphere; always had been. From the time they were young he'd known she'd be a star one day. He scrubbed a hand over his face and pulled out his cell when it buzzed in his pocket. He saw the message was from Van, quickly answered before pocketing his phone again. It had been a hell of a long day. Draining.

But being with Rebel now had pulled everything back into focus. Even if he felt out of control with her, it was still the best kind of chaos.

Because there was nowhere else he'd rather be and no one else he'd rather be with. It had been like that since they were kids. There'd been a revolving door of men at that place, something he hadn't understood at first until his aunt had gently explained things to him.

So Margaret and he had welcomed her over to their place almost twenty-four seven. Of course their house had basically had an open-door policy with all the neighborhood kids being welcome. She'd taught half of them at some point so everyone knew her.

"What?" Weston blinked when he realized Rebel had said something and everyone was looking at him.

"I was just telling them how your aunt gave me my first guitar and managed to get me music lessons for free." Rebel was smiling at him as if he hung the moon as she continued. "And Weston booked me my very first gig at a little dive bar in Coral Gables. Called in a favor to a friend right before he left for boot camp."

"Oh my god," Nancy, one of the new hires, gushed. "That's amazing."

"Yep. If it wasn't for him or his aunt, I don't know where I'd be." She stared at him as she spoke and there was something in her dark amber eyes he felt all the way to his marrow. No amount of fame or money would ever change the connection between them. And today of all days he wondered if maybe—

Rebel's phone started ringing, and the moment was broken as she glanced down at the screen.

"I've got to leave in a few but if you all want a couple pictures, let me know," she said, to the delight of his staff.

Ten minutes later she strode back to him, a grin on her face. God, that smile lit up entire stadiums and it was easy to see why. She was beyond talented, but she also had an electric energy and when she smiled at him, he felt as if he could do absolutely anything. She made him want to be the best version of himself. "Thank you for doing this," he murmured.

The staff had mostly cleaned up the kitchen by now but were still lingering and looking at their phones—and likely posting pictures of her on their social media feeds. He hated that shit but understood it was a necessity for her business. His own too, apparently.

"Want a selfie with me?" she asked, her tone sly.

"What's that look?"

"Nothing. Just asking if Mr. Terrifying wants a picture with me."

"You're not going to start calling me that," he grumbled, his mouth curving up again. Around her it was like he couldn't help but smile.

"Fine. But come here." She held out her phone and slid up next to him, moving in close.

Her coconut vanilla scent teased him, made it hard to think as she tugged him down to her. Yep, she was small but she was definitely the boss. Because he'd do any damn thing this woman asked.

"Come on, that's not a smile."

Hell, he was supposed to be taking a picture with her, but he was always distracted around her. And when she was so close, her tight body pressed up against his, he was having a hard time *not* imagining that they were both naked and pressed up against each other. He glanced at her phone screen and started to smile when she suddenly kissed his cheek as she snapped the image.

He blinked, electricity punching through him even as she made a pleased sound as she looked at the picture. "Send that to me," he managed to rasp out even as he felt the kiss of her lips on his cheek all the way to his core.

"Do you care if I post this online?" she asked as she texted him the image.

That was going to be his screensaver for the rest of time. "Do whatever you want." *Post it on the Jumbotron in Madison Square Garden. Or send it to that handsome prick Anthony who's in all your social media photos.* He blinked when he realized she was staring up at him. Wait, had he said all that aloud? "What?" Hell, he needed to start paying attention. Normally he was aware of his surroundings at all times. Hazard of his former job and hell, what he did now.

But Rebel had a way of making everything else around them disappear simply by being close to him.

"You just looked a little murdery."

"Is that a word?"

She lifted a shoulder, grinned. "I don't know but... I've got to go. My driver's waiting out back. He just texted." She made a face and sighed.

Weston frowned. "I'll take you wherever you need to go."

"I appreciate the offer, but no. I... sort of ditched my driver and normal bodyguard for tonight. But my agent is annoyed and she's right. I need to get home and rest for tomorrow night. I've got a busy day tomorrow."

There was a hell of a lot he wanted to say—like *stay. Come home with me.* But he just nodded and pulled her into a tight hug, wishing he had the *right* to ask her to come home with him. He buried his face against the top of her head, tried not to inhale too deeply, but he was high on this woman. "Thank you for being with me today. You made a shitty day a lot easier to deal with."

"Don't make me cry again," she murmured against his chest and hell, he never wanted to let her go.

But he forced himself to walk her to the back door where, sure enough, there was her driver and a bodyguard with a logo on his shirt that he vaguely recognized. He wanted to tell Rebel that she should be using Red Stone Security for her needs while she was in Miami—and anywhere, for that matter—but kept that thought to himself.

*For now.*

He opened the door for her when the bodyguard made a move to. "Text me when you've made it home?" he asked as she slid into the back seat of the SUV with dark-tinted windows. At least no one would be able to see her in the back.

"Definitely. You uh... doing anything else tonight?"

He frowned. "It's ten and I'm an old man." And he'd just buried his aunt today. He was heading home and crashing.

She shook her head, but leaned back in her seat. "I'll talk to you soon."

He stepped back and shut the door, ignoring the ache in his chest as she was driven away. He wished... well, he wished a lot of things.

Didn't mean they were ever going to happen.

Not when Rebel only saw him as a friend and always would.

# CHapter 4

Rebel stared at the picture of her and Weston, glad that her assigned bodyguard was in the front seat with the driver instead of in the back with her.

Not that she really cared if a stranger saw the picture, but she didn't want anyone else looking at this. It was just for her. And these days, so many things weren't simply hers anymore. She so badly wanted to post the picture of her and Weston on her social media but knew if she did, that it would open him up to speculation and media scrutiny.

That was something she wouldn't do. She knew he valued his privacy and it wasn't like he'd signed up for her crazy world. They were just friends, though she wanted more. Always had. Some teeny-tiny, petty part of her had wanted to post it so Elliana could see, but then she felt like a gigantic *monster* for being like that. Good god, this whole jealousy thing had to stop.

Even if he'd been with the woman, or was currently seeing her, or whatever, it wasn't Rebel's business. He would always be her friend no matter what. He'd been a rock for her when she'd been dealing with the never-ending drama from her mother, and then when he'd been overseas, she knew she'd been a rock for him. He'd told her so more than once. And maybe this lifelong bond would have to be enough, no matter how much she wanted more.

As she stared at the picture like a total teenager, her phone buzzed in her hand. She smiled when she saw Anthony's name. "Hey," she said. They'd been friends almost since the beginning of her career. He'd lifted her up when he'd been a way bigger star than her and man, that was something she'd never forget.

"Hey boo."

She laughed lightly. "Are we already into the champagne?" An easy guess since she could hear loud music in the background and had no doubt he was at some club. He loved dancing and all the Miami clubs reserved a spot for him in their VIP sections. He was very good for business.

"Yep. And I wanted to let you know that I'm *officially* coming out tonight."

She blinked in surprise. "As in…"

"As in, Insta official."

"Aww, I'm so glad. Is Bailey ready for this?" Bailey was Anthony's boyfriend, though they'd never been seen in public together. Anthony's jackass label wanted him to keep his relationship quiet even though it was 2023. And though she couldn't prove it, she was pretty sure they were the ones who sent all those pictures of her and Anthony to various tabloids with insinuations that they were together.

Not that either of them minded. If they were linked together, it kept people from speculating about their romantic lives and offered them both some protection. A sort of easy buffer from crap.

"Baby girl, he's been ready for this for a long time. And I finally realized that you can't love someone in private. Not truly. He deserves to be with someone who's proud enough to hold his hand in public and claim him for the world to see. And I'm tired of living a half-life. I just wanted to let you know in case you get questions about it before the concert tomorrow."

"As soon as you post it on Insta, I'm going to be the first comment of congratulations. So that should answer any questions about how I feel."

"You know it won't be enough. People are still going to ask you for your opinion, want more details."

She groaned, knowing it was true. For some reason, people wanted to know every little thing about celebrities. Even benign shit. The last article she'd willingly read about herself had been about her clothes. She could almost quote the damn thing because it was so stupid.

*Rebel rocks a classic Channel cardigan with Gucci jeans and daring heels as she goes shoe shopping with bestie. The native Miami singer wore her brunette tresses in a chic updo. She added some sparkle with sapphire earrings, gold bangles and her classic '70s style sunglasses.*

Seriously, who caaaaaared? Ugh.

"I'm posting now," he said.

She held her phone out, grinned at the picture that popped up of Anthony kissing Bailey, a bright, familiar Miami nightclub in the background. She commented with a ton of hearts and other emojis and captioned it: *My two favorite guys! Love you both!*

"You're the best," Anthony murmured, then sighed.

"I know. So what's up?"

"Nothing. Just... I know I'll have to deal with a lot of hate online, but—"

"Ignore it. Who gives a shit what those assholes think? If they don't listen to your music from now on, so what? You know they're just lying anyway, because you're awesome, and who's going to give up listening to you?"

"And this is why you're my best friend. Also, I'm a terrible best friend because I just realized what you've been doing today. How's Weston? And how are you?"

"I'm okay. Same with him... I had dinner with him tonight." And she couldn't keep the wistfulness out of her voice.

"Ah." The decibel of the noise got quieter and she guessed he's ducked into an alcove or something. "So are you ever going to admit your feelings to him?"

"Ugh."

"That's not an answer."

"It's the only one I've got. Now go, enjoy your sweet man. I'm almost home and I've got to get some sleep before tomorrow morning. You know Paige is going to be there at the crack of dawn." Her agent went in manic mode on concert days and while Rebel was grateful, she always had to mentally prepare for the whirlwind that was Paige.

He just snickered. "All right. But I might stop by tomorrow."

"Please do, you know you're welcome anytime. Both of you. I'll double check with the main gate but the security should have you down as an approved guest. Give Bailey my love."

"He's blowing kisses to you right now."

Laughing despite the heaviness still weighing on her chest, she ended the call and pulled up the picture of her and Weston again.

She wasn't sure she'd ever get over her feelings for him. But they'd been friends for so damn long that if he was into her, he'd have made a move or at least let her know in some way. No way a man like Weston wouldn't go for what he wanted.

So she was going to do what she always did and bury her feelings down deep. If she didn't put herself out there, she wouldn't get hurt. For so many years she'd been desperate for her mom's love and affection. Eventually—though it took longer than she wanted to admit—Rebel had realized her mother wasn't capable of caring for her in the way she needed. So she'd learned to bury everything as a second nature.

Knowing he was likely on his way home, she called Weston, wanting to hear his voice again even though she'd just seen him. Because the man was her addiction.

"Hey, everything okay?" His voice was tense as he answered.

"Yeah, yeah. I forgot to mention earlier that I got you backstage passes, you know, if you wanted to come to the concert tomorrow." She winced, then wondered if that was egotistical. Or desperate. Jesus, his aunt had just died. "Not that I expect—"

"I've got tickets. A bunch of people from work are going too."

"I can get everyone backstage passes then."

"Oh, no, that's too much."

"Well what's the point of being the boss bitch if I can't give out backstage passes to people I like?"

He laughed lightly. "Okay. I just don't want to put you out."

"And I'm going to pretend you *didn't* just say that. Are you sure the concert won't be too late for your old man sensibilities?"

He laughed even harder. "No promises."

"Oh my god, we're literally the same age!" They'd both just turned thirty a couple months ago, within weeks of each other.

"What can I say, I need my beauty sleep more than you."

She started to respond when the driver cursed loudly and—*crunch*.

Rebel cried out when she flew forward, the seatbelt jerking her back into place under the impact of the crash. Ooooh, her driver had just rear-ended someone. But then she spotted a photographer getting out of the car and realized the asshole had likely caused it to take pictures of her.

"What's wrong?" Weston demanded.

"Ah, we were just in a little fender bender." She scrubbed a hand over her face as tension built inside her. This was definitely going to be a *thing* with pictures blasted everywhere.

Didn't matter that she hadn't been driving. And it didn't matter that she was pretty sure the driver from the car in front of them currently taking pictures had done this intentionally. Police would have to be called and the headlines were going to write themselves.

"Ms. Martinez, stay in the car, please," her bodyguard said before he slid out of the passenger side.

The driver did as well, both shutting her inside the relative quiet.

"What?" she asked, realizing Weston was saying something.

"Where are you?" From his tense tone, she guessed he might have asked more than once.

"Oh, ah... I don't know." She glanced around the neighborhood, saw mostly darkened businesses. Up ahead she could see a busy street and realized her driver had been taking a shorter, less traffic-filled route. "Oh, I see now. I'm not too far from home at least."

"Rebel." His tone was harder than it normally was. "Drop me a pin. I'm coming to you now."

She blinked. "You don't need to do that."

"Rebel."

Sighing, she did as he said, but continued, "Look, the cops are no doubt going to be here soon and my driver is currently talking to the asshole who slammed on his brakes in front of us... Ah, crap."

"What?"

"A few more cars just pulled up behind us," she muttered. "Definitely photographers. This was a setup."

"I'll be there in seven minutes."

"Weston, you're so sweet, but you don't need to do this. Hey, my agent is calling and I need to answer. Don't come here!" She hung up, not waiting for an answer. She didn't want Weston tangled up in any of her life's insanity.

He'd made his billions about a year before she'd really started topping the charts on a consistent basis. But unlike her, he was never in the spotlight. Not really. Sometimes his company was, and he and his business partners had once been featured on the cover of *Forbes*, but it wasn't the same level of scrutiny she dealt with. Though he had been in the business headlines recently because his company was talking to Red Stone Security about some top-secret deal. But other than his company, he had absolutely no social media presence. None of the people he worked with did.

"Hey, Paige," she said to her agent.

"Hey, I just saw you were at some Italian restaurant tonight."

"Ah, yeah, you know that. I told you."

"Well yeah, but I didn't know you were doing a photo shoot."

"I *didn't*. I took a few selfies with some of the people who worked there. My driver was just in a fender bender and I'm currently hunkered down in the backseat ignoring camera flashes outside the car."

"What! Hold on." Paige started barking orders at someone, her voice slightly muffled. Then she came back on the line. "I've got a new driver on his way to you. Four minutes out. Don't wait for the cops. Get in the new car and get the hell out of there."

"Paige—"

"No. Listen to me. I... didn't want to say anything until after the final show, but you've gotten some new letters. More than normal, and not the usual 'marry me' crap. I want you home and safe asap."

"Okay." Rebel's stomach tightened as she imagined what was in the letters. For the most part she always had a guard with her and only posted pictures of her outings long after she'd left somewhere. But she'd had concerts all over the country the last six months, so everyone knew she was going to be at those. And she'd been receiving some seriously creepy messages lately.

Enough that they worried Paige, and that woman was normally unflappable.

"Okay what?" Paige pressed.

"I'll leave when the driver shows up."

"Good. And Rodrigo is going with you. I just texted him."

"Okay." Rodrigo, her current bodyguard, was nice enough, but he was super quiet and had made it clear that he didn't want to chitchat. Which was fine. He was just being a professional, but it was a little off-putting.

"I see on my map that he's pulling down your street. You know the deal. Go as soon as Rodrigo deems it safe."

Rebel could hear sirens in the distance, closed her eyes even as she said, "Yep." Then she texted Weston and told him he didn't want to be here for this shitshow. As she finished hitting send, Rodrigo opened her door, grabbed her purse and shielded her with his body as he hurried her through the throng of photographers. Quiet or not, the man was really good at his job because people backed up for him.

She kept her face down, not looking at any of them, and definitely not answering any questions, but was still semi-blinded by the wild flashes. Jesus.

Normally Miami was her safe haven, but someone must have leaked where she'd be tonight because this bullshit was definitely coordinated. And disappointing. But it was what it was.

At least that was what she tried to tell herself as she slid into the backseat of the waiting SUV and shoved out a relieved breath as the door shut behind her, muting the shouted questions about Anthony and his new boyfriend.

They really hadn't wasted any time, had they. Ugh.

"I'm going to need to talk to the cops," she said to Rodrigo, who was talking quietly into his phone from the front seat, likely to Paige, she guessed.

He paused and looked back at her. "My brother-in-law works for the PD. I'm reaching out now to let them know that you'll happily talk to them, but we decided to move you because of an active threat."

"Oh. Thank you." Sighing, she laid her head back against the seat, wondering if anyone was following, and deciding not to turn around and find out.

Her neighborhood was private, one of the reasons she'd bought there. They had a strict policy about nonresidents or approved guests because some very wealthy people as well as other celebrities lived there. Right now she was damn glad she had her safe haven to go to.

She glanced down at her phone, her heart rate kicking up a bit when she saw Weston's name.

*You okay?* he asked.

*Yeah. They got me out of there pretty fast. I'm going to go home and crash.*

*Want me to come over?*

The question surprised her, and she so desperately wanted to say yes. But she simply didn't feel right about dragging him into the chaos that was her life now.

*I appreciate the offer, but no. I'll see you tomorrow though after the concert?*

*I'll be seeing you before then.*

She wanted to ask what he meant, but got a barrage of texts from Anthony and others and tried to keep up as she answered all of them.

Eventually she silenced all the alerts on her phone and didn't bother checking social media. She didn't want to deal with anything else until tomorrow.

She especially didn't want to deal with the creepy letters she'd been receiving lately. Of course she'd have to, but for now she was going to block out the rest of the world.

# CHAPTER 5



*Eight years ago*

Weston! I'm headlining my own show tonight and can hardly believe it. I've done too many shows to count in the last few years that they're all starting to blur, but this is the first one I'm headlining. Oh and this super famous country singer bought one of my songs, which is wild to even write. I'll tell you who when we see each other in person next. Speaking of, when will that be? (Imagine my whining voice). I haven't been back to Miami in ten months but Aunt Margaret has been keeping all my things for me. She's the best. I'd looked into buying a small condo but she told me to save my money. And she's right, I'd have ended up having to have someone look after the place. Eventually I want to buy a place but maybe that's just a pipe dream for now.

Oh, this guy Anthony (a singer and performer) also asked me to do a couple duets with him. He said he saw me years ago and liked my style. I'm stunned he asked for me when he's a much bigger name but my agent is really excited about this. She thinks it's a big step in my career. So much is happening at once that it feels like a blur. And a dream. I can hardly believe it.

What are you up to? How's California treating you? Is it different than being on the East Coast? When are you coming home to Miami? Give me all the details! I miss you.

xo,
Rebel

***

Rebel,

I saw some of your videos online and you're amazing. I can still see you singing when we were kids in Aunt Margaret's backyard but now it's in front of thousands. Not surprised you're headlining. It's about time! Can't wait to hear who you sold a song to.

California's okay but I'm not actually there anymore. Got deployed again and didn't have time to tell you. My time to reup is coming up soon and I don't know if I'll do it. I've been thinking about getting out, but I might do one more tour and then get out. Who knows at this point. I heard we might get sent to Japan next and if we do, I'll probably reup for a while. But I've been working on something with Van, Elliana and a few others. We have this idea for when we get out… I'll tell you more about it in person. Right now everything is too up in the air but as soon as I have leave, I'm going to see Aunt Margaret. She came out to visit me in California a month ago and said she loved it, but that she missed her home. Oh, did you hear that Tag and Molly from the old neighborhood got married? He did his eight years and decided not to reup his next contract. They're settling back in Miami apparently, so hopefully next time we're both in town we can get together with them too. I miss you.

—Weston

# CHAPTER 6

"Thank you for meeting us here." Weston kept his tone neutral as the chef of his restaurant stepped into the kitchen to meet with him, his manager, Bianca, and one of his attorneys, Catarina. He wasn't sure who was the more intimidating of the two women. There was also a notary and extra witness for what was about to happen next.

Aldo, a young up-and-coming chef who Weston had heard only good things about, frowned as he looked between Weston and Bianca. It was seven in the morning, too early for anyone to be here yet. "Didn't sound like I had much of a choice. What's going on?"

"You're fired, that's what's going on." Weston could barely keep the rage out of his voice. After showing up to the scene of the fender bender last night, and seeing Rebel being whisked away by her bodyguard, seeing in person the nightmare of photographers hounding her, he'd been out for blood, wanting to know who had set her up.

Because it was clear she'd been followed from the restaurant. There had been far too many people there so quickly. And that meant someone on his own staff had tipped them off.

Catarina cleared her throat and shot Weston a sharp look, silently telling him to shut up. Which, fine, he knew he should do. It was taking all his self-control not to lay the guy flat on the tile right now and knock his teeth in.

"What?" Aldo's eyes widened.

"We're offering you a severance that I personally don't think you deserve," Catarina said. "Not after you leaked Rebel Martinez's whereabouts last night to the press before she left here."

"I did no such—"

"I'm going to stop you right there." Catarina was a tall blonde with icy green eyes and an incredibly sharp mind. She'd left her old law firm when they kept passing her over for partner and now was one of the most sought-after lawyers in Miami—and the southeast. She'd brought in forty percent of her old firm's money and had taken all her clients when she'd left. "We know you did. Phone records don't lie."

Aldo's face tightened. "You have no right—"

Catarina held up a finger, made a little tsking sound. "Stop. Talking. If you ever want to work in this town again, you will listen carefully." She held out a manila envelope. "This is what we're offering you as a severance and you will sign off on it and agree to never litigate with or harass my client, and my client will offer you a neutral recommendation, only verifying that you worked here."

With shaking hands, Aldo pulled out the papers and frowned. "This isn't enough—"

"It's all we're offering, and I'm two goddamn seconds from pulling it," Weston snapped. "You were paid well, asshole. And when you signed the contract to work here, you agreed in writing to never deal with the press when it came to celebrity clients. We shouldn't even be offering you a severance." But his attorney thought it was the smart move, guaranteed to ensure the man had no legal leg to stand on later if he decided to sue for wrongful termination. Especially since Weston had gotten the guy's phone records illegally.

"No one got hurt," Aldo snapped, flipping over to the signature page and, to Weston's surprise, grabbing a pen from his pocket and scrawling his signature. "And this place is going to fail without me."

Weston snorted at the man's ego, but managed to keep his mouth shut as the jerk handed everything back to Catarina. And he remained silent as the notary and witnesses finished up. Honestly, he deserved a goddamn medal for not knocking the smug look off Aldo's face.

For a moment, Aldo looked as if he might say more to Weston but whatever the chef saw on Weston's face stopped him cold. He looked at Catarina instead, gave her a curt nod, then stalked out the back door.

"What a prick," Bianca snarled. "I never would have thought he'd done it either."

Weston didn't respond as he shoved through the kitchen door into the empty restaurant.

No surprise, Catarina followed him. "We talked about this. It's the right move."

"The right move would have been knocking that prick on his ass."

The woman sighed then took a seat at the bar. "I tell my ten-year-old that violence isn't the answer but in this case, it would have been justified."

He blinked at her. "Seriously?"

"I mean, *no*, because then he'd have sued you for sure. Or maybe I should have let you because then I'd have gotten to bill you for all those hours." The grin she gave him was pure Catarina.

He snorted and slid around the bar, pulled out a couple bottles of water, sparkling for her. "I don't like that he got a severance package at all."

"No one decent is going to hire him now. You talked to enough restaurant owners last night and this morning—before he signed off on the package—that word will spread. You know his career here is essentially over. Maybe he'll start his own place, but who cares? No one will trust him again and, in this town…" She shrugged.

"It would have felt really good to punch him is all I'm saying."

"Take the win. He's young and stupid and he's going to implode. Trust me, I've seen the type. He was so damn arrogant that he didn't even think of having an attorney look over that paperwork. And he really, really should have." The grin she gave then was scary. But she slid off the barstool and picked up her bag and bottle of water. "By chance if you have extra tickets to any of Rebel's concerts, I would be a hero to my children."

He blinked in surprise. "Really?"

She rolled her eyes. "Oh yeah. Neither me nor my ex could get tickets to her upcoming shows, so if you could manage to get me three tickets, I'd owe you."

"Done. And I might be able to get you backstage passes."

Her eyes widened. "And now you're my favorite client."

Laughing, he just shook his head and hoped Rebel didn't mind giving him a few more passes. He actually had the extra tickets already, had bought a bundle of them for people at work—he wanted everyone to see her brilliance. Since not everyone could go, he had about five left.

He walked her out and locked the front door behind her, then made another call. He had one more stop before he headed to Rebel's. After what he'd seen online this morning, it was clear that Rebel and Anthony weren't an item and had likely never been.

If Rebel was single, he was done waiting.

He was going to take his chance and if he got shot down, well, then nothing had changed.

***

*Buzz me in.*

Rebel read the text from Weston, frowned as she replied. *You're here?* How had he gotten past the security gate?

*Yep. And I have gifts.*

She pulled up the security feed on her phone, saw him sitting in a golf cart by her front gate. She pressed the open button and hurried from her room all the way to the front of the house. Still in her hot pink robe and her hair pulled up into a towel since she'd started an oil treatment, she didn't bother changing. He'd seen her in worse.

"I thought you were resting." Paige looked up as Rebel hurried through the huge kitchen.

"I am." Anticipation buzzed through her, as it always did before she saw Weston. Before she reached the door, she remembered the pink under-eye masks she had on and quickly peeled them off, tucked them into her robe pockets. "Hey," she said after tugging the heavy door open.

"Hey yourself." His grin was slow, almost wicked.

And definitely knee-weakening. His short hair was lightly windblown, likely from riding the golf cart here, and his Henley T-shirt molded to biceps she wanted to nibble on.

Her house was tucked back from the road and she had a huge fence and tons of foliage surrounding her house to give her privacy. The back was truly stunning but none of that mattered as she smiled up at Weston. "What are you doing here? *How* are you here?" Because their security was no joke. He was an approved guest but they still would have alerted her. She glanced past him, eyeing the golf cart as something clicked into place.

"I bought a house in the neighborhood a few months ago." He grinned as he stepped inside, something about him completely different this morning. He seemed... She wasn't sure, but there was a different sort of energy rolling off him.

"Oh my gosh, and you didn't tell me?" She knew exactly which one too because it was gorgeous and had an even better view of the water than hers did. And it was only four houses away.

"I'd planned to surprise you, then time got away from me." He held out a cup of something for her, as well as a pink pastry bag with purple stripes. She didn't recognize the logo but whatever was inside smelled amazing.

She inhaled the to-go cup and smiled. "Hot chocolate?"

"I figured it was a safe bet."

"Always. And I can't believe you're here. Come on." She grabbed his free hand and tugged him to the kitchen, where Paige and Rebel's assistant Anna were going over some things.

They both eyed Weston for a moment, but then immediately went back to what they were doing, thankfully.

"We leave in three hours," Paige said without looking up from her tablet.

As if she didn't know. But Rebel smiled as she grabbed some plates and utensils for them. "I know, Paige." Then to Weston, she said, "We can eat these on the lanai and you can tell me about your new move."

He took the array of things from her and followed her through the maze of her mansion. Some days it was still hard to believe that this place was hers. As they reached the oversized French doors that led to her favorite area, she winced as they passed a large framed photo of her in concert in New York City.

She glanced up at him, anxiety punching through her as she saw him staring at it. "I know, it's embarrassing."

"Embarrassing? It's amazing." His gaze was heated when he looked down at her. Um... what was happening? "*You* are amazing. And performing there was one of your dreams. This is an incredible shot of you." His gaze strayed back to the image of her in a sparkly silver dress reminiscent of Tina Turner, one of her idols.

She was singing a high note, sweat visible across her brow as she belted it out and okay, she did look amazing. Happy in a way she only ever was when singing. "Thanks," she murmured, suddenly feeling awkward and second guessing that look he'd just given her. There was no heat, just her own projections.

So she opened the back doors into her oasis. She had a huge freeform pool with a raised spa, a swim-up bar, a ridiculously large pool house and there was bright foliage everywhere, making the tropical backyard feel magical. "You feel like swimming this morning? It's heated." She sat at the eight-person table and waited as he set everything out, including a spinach croissant, one of her favorites.

This man really did know her.

Normally she only ate high-protein food before a concert but she was keyed up and planned to get in a swim before leaving anyway.

"I don't have my swim trunks." He sat next to her, stretching his long legs out, and she had to tear her gaze away from him.

"You could just wear your birthday suit." She wasn't sure where that had come from but she could almost swear something crackled in the air between them.

Or maybe that was wishful thinking. She gave him a cheeky grin as he blinked at her.

"So, you bought a house here? How do you like it and when do I get to see it?" she asked hurriedly.

"I love it and I'm happy to be so close to you." The way he said that sent ribbons of heat curling through her.

"I'm glad you're so close too. Especially since I'm taking a little break after this." She glanced over her shoulder, though she knew they were alone. She'd already told Paige but hadn't mentioned anything to her assistant. Not that it would truly matter, but she didn't want to deal with questions from anyone right now.

"That's good, right?" His gaze was almost speculative.

"I hope so. I have some ideas for a new album and I just need the break. I've been killing myself the last few years. I got an offer to do a residency in Vegas too."

"Think you'll take it?"

"No. Not now anyway. Probably never, though I don't like to limit myself."

She wasn't sure if it was her imagination but he seemed almost relieved by that.

"I saw that Anthony is in a new relationship. How are you doing?"

She blinked in surprise at the question. "What do you mean? I'm happy for him. Other than you, he's one of my best friends."

"So you two weren't...together?" There was an unexpected note of caution in his tone.

She snort-laughed, unable to stop herself. "Um, no! Wait, you thought I was dating him?" She and Weston might not talk all the time but they texted constantly and she'd have told him if she'd been dating Anthony.

Weston lifted a broad shoulder. "All the tabloids linked you guys together over the years, speculating about it."

"I would have *told* you if I was dating him. Or anyone." And she wondered if he'd tell her. As far as she knew he wasn't dating anyone but that couldn't be right. Just, no way. He was too gorgeous and funny not to be out there playing the field or whatever the hell it was called. "And now you and the whole world know that I'm not his type anyway. But I adore his boyfriend and I'm glad they're finally official. Oh, they'll both be at the concert tonight. He's got a TV appearance late tonight but said he'd stop by before the show."

"I need to tell you something." He shifted slightly, his expression turning serious. "Last night... with the photographers—"

"Oh, it's fine. I already talked to the police about it. They were really nice too. Other than some stupid articles, nothing is going to come of it."

"It's not that. I discovered that the chef who *used* to work at my restaurant, leaked your location to a photog intentionally. I paid him a small severance in exchange for him not making anything a litigious matter between us. But I swear I'm going to personally make sure he doesn't work in this town again."

She blinked at the savagery in his tone. There was something about the protectiveness in his expression that went straight to her core. "Weston... it's fine. I mean, it sucks, but well, people suck. You don't need to worry about that guy or whatever he does in the future."

"You could have been injured last night." And forget about savage. His expression was straight-up murderous now.

She blinked, realizing how angry he truly was, so she stood and took his hand in hers. "I'm more than fine. Come on." He didn't ask questions as she led him to one of the oversized, cushioned chairs on the pool deck.

Or maybe the thing couldn't even be considered a chair. It was the size of a small bed. "You need to breathe for a minute."

As they stretched out together, he wrapped an arm around her and, against her better sense, she cuddled up against him. When they were teens they'd cuddled together watching movies but things had shifted later. Laying like this with him now... she wished it was like this all the time.

"Are you really not upset by last night?" he asked her.

"I'm not happy but I've realized there are some things I can change, and some I can't. So I can't spend a ton of energy worrying about the latter."

"You're a better person than me," he murmured. "Do you ever regret your fame?"

"No." Her answer was immediate. "Because I get to sing and if I'm being really honest, I've got security and if I get sick, I'm not worried about losing my life savings to pay hospital bills. I probably push myself too hard because there's a fear that I could lose it all one day but... no. I don't regret it." Being able to pay her bills, being able to own something, being able to actually help others and use her voice for good things... all that mattered. The fame part, not at all. But she'd put herself out there and tried to make a career out of the thing she loved so no, no regrets.

"Good." He was quiet, but she could feel the steady beat of his heart under her ear as she laid her head on his chest.

If she could, she'd bottle up this moment forever.

"So I found out you were keeping a secret from me." His voice was a little deeper as he spoke into the quiet.

"Secret?" Wait, did he know how she felt about him?

"You bought Aunt Margaret a condo up in Destin. I discovered it when I was going through some of her paperwork."

She let out a laugh. "Oh yeah. I tried to pay off her mortgage once I started making money, but of course you already had. So then I tried to buy her a new house, but she wasn't having any of that. Said she'd never leave the neighborhood. So I bought her a place near her best friend so she could visit throughout the year."

"I wish I'd thought of that," he grumbled, making her laugh again.

Sighing, she curled up against him, but paused when she heard a familiar voice calling out her name. "Uh oh, we have company." She sat up at the sound of Anthony calling her name. He was on her permanent list of people she allowed into the neighborhood and security probably hadn't even bothered to call her.

Both he and Bailey were still wearing what they'd been wearing in the picture from Insta last night and holding cups of what was likely coffee. They both had way more stamina than her. She'd given up trying to keep up with him years ago.

"Well hello," Anthony said with a growing grin as Weston sat up next to her. "Am I interrupting something?"

"What? No!" She adjusted her robe, feeling her cheeks warm, and wanted to smack Anthony. "Don't be ridiculous."

Weston stood and, to her surprise, shook Anthony's hand, then clapped him on the shoulder. "Congrats on making things official." His tone was so damn sincere and he looked so... was relieved the right word?

What the hell was going on with him?

"Thanks." Anthony shook his hand, grinning. "So, you going to the concert tonight?"

"Yep. And tomorrow."

"Good. We can all ride together," Anthony said as he slung an arm around Bailey's shoulders.

"Sounds good to me." Weston was eyeing Anthony in the most curious way.

"Ah..." She looked between the two of them.

Bailey groaned and took a sip of his coffee, didn't bother removing his sunglasses. "I'm never drinking again," he muttered and headed for the big cushion they'd just vacated.

"Are you guys hungry?" she asked. "Weston brought over some treats."

"Starving. Baby, are you hungry? I'll make you a plate," Anthony said.

"Just leave me to my misery." Bailey covered his face with one of the pillows.

"I've got a good hangover remedy. Mind if I use your kitchen?" Weston asked.

"Of course not. Make yourself at home." *Or better yet, make this your home.* Ugh, she was so pathetic.

"Sooooooo." Anthony drawled out the word once it was just the three of them.

Rebel ignored him and returned to the box of pastries and her barely touched croissant. "So what are you doing over here so early?"

"Did he stay the night?" Anthony whispered as he sat across from her, snagging one of the muffins and pulling only the top off to eat.

"No, but he lives in my neighborhood now. He bought the Estevez house from a few doors down."

Anthony waggled his eyebrows. "I like the sound of that. It means you're finally going to get some of that delicious—"

"I can hear you," Bailey growled, his pillow still over his face.

Which just made Rebel snicker. "Please stop now."

"Fine. And we're here because we wanted to use your pool today since mine is still under renovation."

"Of course. I've already told you to just stay here until they're done." She had enough rooms.

He just shrugged in that very Anthony way of his. "I don't want to be a bother."

She wanted to tell him that he wasn't, but this was a conversation they'd had multiple times. "So are you nervous about the interview tonight?"

"A little but..." He shrugged. "My tour is coming up fast."

"Is that why you've been partying so hard?"

"Yep. Gotta get it all out of my system because it's going to be no play for months after this."

"There will be a little play." Bailey finally joined them, sitting next to Anthony but not touching the food.

Anthony glanced at him and the look of pure adoration in his gaze punched her right in the gut.

She was beyond happy for her friend, but she wanted that too. But not with just anyone, with Weston.

The man who was currently making a hangover remedy for one of her best friends, the man she'd known since before she even understood her feelings for him. The man... who now lived very, very close to her.

With him so close... she was thinking about making some very bad or very good decisions once this tour was over.

# CHAPTER 7

*Five years ago*

Weston!

I just read an article about your new company and how you're making waves. That magazine cover of you and your partners was absolute fire. You should totally frame it. How is it being back in Miami? Maybe don't tell me because I miss it so much. Kidding, tell me everything. Are you working too much? Not that I have room to judge, but Aunt Margaret might have snitched on you and said you're barely sleeping. I get it though, because my new motto is that I can sleep when I'm dead, ha.

To answer your last question, this tour is absolutely wild in the best way possible. Headlining is everything I ever imagined. Better even! Also, my agent said that my label wants to funnel a huge marketing campaign that's supposed to do big things for me. It also helps that I already have a solid social media presence but she said this kind of money is unheard of for someone at my level. So anything they ask, I'm doing it. Which of course means I won't be home anytime soon. But I swear next time I am (which will probably be for a concert), I hope we can get together. Aunt Margaret came to see me up in Orlando when I was performing a couple months ago with her best friend. I gave them backstage passes and a bunch of merch and they were the absolute cutest wearing Rebel T-shirts. I posted the picture online and it's probably my most liked picture ever.

How's your new place? And how's the new office? I saw the picture in *Forbes* and it looked impressive. How are Elliana and Van? And what about Molly and Tag? I couldn't make her most recent baby shower but I sent a gift. They seem so adult it's a little terrifying. Having babies and buying a house and all that jazz. She said they were also buying a pet shelter that was about to go under. Have you seen them at all since being back? Tell me everything! I miss you.

xo,
Rebel

***

Rebel,

Aunt Margaret has that picture of you, her and her best friend framed and proudly shows it off to everyone. She's so proud of you. And so am I, in case I don't say it enough. I also put a framed picture of you and I up at work and have all the street cred in the world now apparently. The interns can't believe I know you. They call me an old man (I'm only twenty-six, WTF) and think it's Photoshopped, much to the amusement of my partners. So next time you're in town, you've got to stop by.

The new company is doing well. We just started talking about doing some partnerships with companies here in Miami but who knows what will come of it. I'm trying not to get too ahead of myself and also remind myself to slow down. Work-life balance or some shit right? It feels like all I do is work. All of us are like that though so at least I'm in good company. And at least I'm not stuck in the desert for months at a time.

I miss you too.
Weston

# CHAPTER 8

"Come in!" Rebel called out as she zipped up her purple sparkly boot. Her first outfit of the night was a shimmery, sequined purple skirt and matching top that showed off her midriff.

When Weston popped his head in, her heart rate kicked up. "Hey." He stepped into her dressing room carrying a bouquet of yellow hibiscus flowers. Her favorite because they looked so happy and attracted butterflies.

"Hey! I'm glad you made it before the concert starts." She'd been here for the last seven hours with everyone as they prepped for the final show.

"Of course. You look gorgeous," he murmured as he set the vase down on a nearby table.

Her assistant Anna popped her head in then, nodded at Weston before addressing Rebel. "Just giving you your half hour reminder," she said with a smile.

"Thanks. Hey, will you make sure those specific flowers make it back to my house? I want them in my kitchen, please."

"Of course. I'll make sure they get transported after the show."

"Thanks." Rebel looked at Weston then, just took in every delicious inch. He had on a black T-shirt—with her face on it that he'd clearly bought from concession or already had—that showed off the ropes of muscles he'd honed to perfection. She never really thought of forearms as sexy but he had some serious forearm and bicep game. "You look pretty good yourself," she said, picking up from his compliment.

His eyes weren't ice blue tonight, but seemed to almost darken as he stalked toward her. Seriously, what was going on with him? She swore something had changed. And she was afraid to lean into it, to admit that maaaaybe he was looking at her with a whole lot of appreciation the past couple days.

"Has it been a madhouse today?" he asked.

"Oh, you have no idea." Laughing lightly, she shook her hips, making the fringe of the purple skirt shimmer around her. "And all my outfits tonight are various colors—all sequin."

"Looks good on you. But everything looks good on you."

Warmth spread through her at his words and she wondered at the heated look in his gaze. Was she imagining it? She was so keyed up right now, the familiar adrenaline before a show punching through her. And it was amplified from having him in her private space. She cleared her throat. "Ah, do you want anything to drink? I've got anything you can imagine." Although she drank only water or hot tea with honey before a show.

"I'm good. Thank you again for all the backstage passes." There was a little frown on his face as he spoke, glanced around the room.

"What's that look?"

"Just wondering where your security is."

"Ah, Rodrigo should be outside."

"I saw him talking to one of your dancers." And Weston's frown was firmly in place.

"And?" She sat on the couch, stretched her legs out as she grabbed her water. Soon she was going to be shaking her hips, singing and dancing with all the energy she had. She always tried to hydrate as much as possible before concerts.

He lifted a shoulder and joined her on the other end of the couch. "You need more security than one guy." The tightly coiled energy rolling off him was palpable as he watched her.

His reaction surprised her. "There's tons of security here at the stadium. But I've found I don't need more than one person."

"You should have two. At least. And I suggest using Red Stone Security."

There was a knock on her door and Rodrigo called out a reminder of the time for her.

She blinked at Weston's tone. "Two seems like overkill."

"Not with a stalker out there."

She sighed, regretting that she'd told him about the weirdo sending her messages. "I've had stalkers before." Something he already knew. It was unfortunately a part of her job. A very creepy part. One had killed himself and the other moved to Australia.

"I don't like how calmly you say that," he growled.

"What's going on with you tonight? You're clearly in a mood." He looked like a caged tiger sitting there.

"Paige let me look at some of the messages you've received. I think you need to take it more seriously."

Rebel straightened and stood. She couldn't believe Paige had let him see that crap. "I *am* taking it seriously. It's why I have a bodyguard and I'm very careful about where I go. And I've got a state-of-the-art security system as well as cameras at the house. I'm almost never alone when working."

"Hell, I'm sorry." He stood, pulled her into his arms. "I'm sorry, Rebel. I know you're smart and looking out for yourself, and I'm a dick for bringing this up now. I just... worry about you." His grip around her tightened.

As he pulled her close, she felt her anger fading as quickly as it had come. She knew he only cared about her, had always worried about her, since they were kids. She melted into his arms, holding him just as close. Even with her heeled boots he was a lot taller than her. She turned her face against his chest, listened to the steady beat of his heart. "I know and I appreciate it. You're always looking out for me." She just wished there was more to it than friendship between them.

"Maybe you could think about using Red Stone Security in the future."

She lightly pinched his side and let out a laugh as she leaned back. "I'll seriously think about it—later. But no more security talk. Not before this show... You know you can hang out in the wings if you want, get a close up of the concert if you'd like. Unless you want to sit with your friends. Oh, or you could invite Anthony and Bailey to hang with you. I know you guys rode together."

Reaching up, he brushed back a strand of hair that had fallen from her high ponytail. And she swore she felt an actual spark between them. Yep, had to be her adrenaline right now. Because she couldn't stop staring at his mouth.

His very kissable lips. Wait, he was saying something.

She blinked, looked up at him. "What?"

"I was just saying that I'll watch from the wings and that you're going to kill it tonight. You're amazing, Rebel." His voice was deep and delicious and oh god, she was having some very non-friend thoughts right now. She also realized his hand was gently cupping her face, his thumb stroking her cheek.

Um... what the hell was happening? Because she liked it way too much. "Thank you," she whispered, her throat tightening as he started to lean down. Her heart went wild against her rib cage. Weston was about to kiss her and she was so here for it. And more.

"Time to go!" Paige stepped into her dressing room, her headset on, a tablet in hand, but blinked at the two of them. "Oh, sorry, Rebel."

Rebel cleared her throat and stepped back, immediately felt the loss of Weston's warmth. He'd been about to kiss her. He definitely had. "I'll see you after the concert?" she asked him. Maybe they could finish what they'd started.

"I'm not going anywhere." Oh, that was definitely heat in his voice, and his gaze.

Either that or she was losing her mind.

Years of longing surfaced, threatening to choke her as she looked into his blue eyes, but she ruthlessly shoved them back down. She had a show to do. "Good. You can stay here as long as you want. Lia's about to start the pre-show and I've got to be out there ready to go when she's done."

He simply nodded, his eyes electric as she hurried off with Paige, immediately going into showtime mode.

But still, in the back of her mind, she couldn't get that look out of her mind, that almost kiss. The way he'd gently cupped her cheek, the way he'd stared at her as if she was the only thing that existed.

Even though she had to shove all her personal stuff to the back of her mind for now, she was going to get Weston alone later. And they were going to finish what he'd started.

***

Weston was aware when Paige slid up next to him as he stood off to the side of the stage, her headset still in place. She was high-strung, but damn good at her job.

"She's incredible," Paige said after clicking the mute button on her headset.

"She really is." Weston couldn't take his eyes off Rebel. She had the kind of stage presence that was simply inborn. She'd honed her talent, had taken voice lessons and could play multiple instruments but watching her out onstage, singing to the huge crowd as if they were the only humans on Earth... Damn.

The emotion of her music wrapped around him, cut through straight to the heart of him. And as he watched her onstage, now in a sparkly gold dress, he remembered the first time she'd performed for him and his aunt. They'd been fourteen and even then, he'd known she was something special. Her mother had told her she was an idiot for thinking she could be a singer, had told her to keep her 'expectations realistic', but not Aunt Margaret.

"You ever going to tell her what you did?" Paige asked, her voice so damn low he almost didn't hear her over Rebel's singing and the chanting of the crowd as they sang along with her.

He shot her a surprised look. "Wasn't planning on it. Why?"

She tilted her head to the side slightly. "I'm just trying to figure you out," she said on a laugh. "You're a strange man. In a good way," she added.

He turned back to watching Rebel even as he wondered why Paige was next to him. She was a tall woman with caramel-colored hair and a commanding voice. And she was very good at her job. Since they were alone, he said, "You need to hire more security for Rebel. I've got contacts with Red Stone." Especially now that he and his partners had just signed an exclusive contract with them. Something that had been years in the making.

"I agree and I've already suggested that to Rebel multiple times."

"You have?" Rebel threw her hands in the air and the pyrotechnics behind her exploded in a flash of gold and greens.

"Yep, but I think my language was too soft. I didn't want to worry her during a tour, but maybe I should have been more forceful."

"Now that she's here in Miami, insist on it. Or just make the change." He planned to bring up her security again later as well. Because he might have made a mistake by mentioning it to Rebel right before she was about to go on, but he was serious about her safety.

"You're very bossy."

"I know." Though usually Van or Elliana told him he was a bulldozer asshole. Same difference.

Someone hurried up to Paige then, whispering something, so she clicked her headset back on and rushed away, snapping out orders in that voice that had people around her doing double takes. Weston ignored her.

Even though he hated taking his gaze away from Rebel, he scanned the stage again out of habit, nodded once to Rodrigo, her personal guard who was about twenty feet away from him. The guy had an impressive background, Weston would give him that much. He'd been in special forces for eight years and had been in the protection business for five. His financials were solid and he was married. Both he and his wife made good money, didn't live outside their means and were involved in their kids' lives. And he had no vices that Weston could find. Didn't mean he wasn't a problem, but the odds were low.

The other man nodded back then looked down at Lia Harris, the woman who'd been opening for Rebel this tour. She was good, but not as good as Rebel.

No one was.

Not that he was biased or anything. He snorted to himself even as his heart rate kicked up watching her onstage. As she began another song, the ground beneath him shook as the crowd stood and started stomping their feet. This was the final song of the night, the first of hers that had gone platinum; the one that had really catapulted her career. It was about love and loss and she'd once told him that she'd written it about her mother, though people always speculated it was about heartbreak. It was, just not the kind people realized.

As she belted out the last of the lyrics, he frowned as the pyrotechnics started up. Two huge parallel bars were set up behind the main stage; directly behind the drummer, guitarist and her. Eighteen attachments total—nine on each bar—shot out small sparks, giving the illusion of fireworks behind them. It was an incredible addition to the show, but something was off. The top bar was shaking slightly, which couldn't be right. The bars were supposed to be secured with bolts.

Suddenly sparks exploded everywhere, out over the drummer and covering some of the people near the back of the stage. The drummer jumped up, shouting out in alarm. And the top railing was shaking even more—something was wrong.

Weston started moving before he realized what he was doing, instinct and years of being in a war zone kicking in. He raced at Rebel, saw her turning to look at him, her eyes wide with shock but out of the corner of his eye, he saw the top railing shuddering even harder.

Someone was shouting something, but he ignored all of it as he reached Rebel and tossed her over his shoulder fireman style. As he did, he heard a hideous snap as something cracked, and then screams as the upper railing snapped free, sending a rain shower of fireworks over the entire stage. He heard a huge crash behind him, didn't turn around again as he reached the other side of the stage, only stopping once he was sure they were out of the danger zone.

"Are you okay?" he asked as he set Rebel on her feet.

"Oh my god," she breathed out, her expression set in horror. Her gaze trailed past him to the stage and ice flooded his veins as he followed her line of sight.

The upper railing had broken free of where it was supposed to be bolted in and whipped out toward the area where she had been standing only moments ago, knocked the drums out of the way completely—he saw the drummer standing safe—and slammed down right where Rebel had been singing. The stage had a huge hole in it where the thing had landed.

The metal beam could have killed her with one hit.

"I should—" She took a step forward, but he grabbed her back as more screams filled the air. This time from the crowd.

"*No.* The fire department will already be on the way. You can't go out there," he growled. Then he shouted, "Everyone off the goddamn stage! And someone turn off the power to the pyrotechnics!" Sparks were still spouting out in places and no one seemed to be doing a damn thing.

Without waiting for a response from anyone, he scooped her up again and carried her deeper into the back as behind them, chaos erupted. He couldn't see Rodrigo anywhere, wondered where the hell her bodyguard was but shelved the thought for now. Her safety was the only thing that mattered. He certainly wasn't going to wait for someone else to take charge.

"Weston—"

"No. I'm taking you to your room." He had to loop them back around the stage through the maze of hallways, but he'd mapped out the concert venue earlier and knew the way.

As they passed people, he shouted at everyone to stay back even as he wondered again where the hell her bodyguard was. Weston was going to have some words with him eventually but for now, his only concern was getting Rebel to the safety of her dressing room.

Once they made it there, he swiped the card she handed him and opened the door. Then he set her on her feet and scanned her from head to toe, his heart rate slowly returning to normal.

"I'm okay." Her hands gently settled on his face and he realized he was trembling. "I promise," she murmured.

He swallowed hard, pulled her into his arms and held her close. "I could have lost you," he rasped out, that ice from before coating his entire body now.

"Well you didn't, and I'm right here."

Jesus, she shouldn't be comforting him, but he couldn't find his voice as he ran his hand up and down her spine.

He wasn't sure if what had happened was an accident or on purpose, but he was damn sure going to find out. And until he knew she was safe, he wasn't letting Rebel out of his sight.

# CHAPTER 9

How the hell had tonight failed?

Rebel was supposed to be dead. Or maimed. Or in a coma.

Just out of the picture.

That bitch had everything and could get anything she wanted.

*Anyone* she wanted.

Or at least it seemed that way. Men fell at her feet. Women tried to copy the way she dressed. It was disgusting.

Tonight was supposed to have changed all that. But now, all the news feeds would talk about how their little darling had escaped being injured.

That rescue stunt by Weston at the last second had ruined everything—he'd moved so damn fast. So unexpectedly.

It would just give Rebel more fame and marketing. Exactly what she didn't deserve.

Stupid whore.

She shouldn't be up onstage for the world to see.

It would be sweet justice to rip everything from her, to watch everything she had burn all around her.

# CHAPTER 10

"Are you sure I can go?" Rebel asked the detective who'd arrived half an hour ago on the scene. She wasn't sure if the Miami PD was treating what happened as an accident or a crime. No one had told her much of anything at this point and it was frustrating.

"Absolutely." Detective Duarte nodded, looked between her and Weston, then continued. "We have a lot to figure out here but we're going to be looking over the security recordings and if it turns out this wasn't an accident, we'll need to talk more. Especially with the influx of hateful messages it sounds like you've received lately. But I think it's best if you go home for now. There are too many people here as it is."

"When you talk to her, it'll be at her house or mine." Weston's expression was as hard as his tone.

The borderline hostility from Weston surprised her, but she liked that he was taking charge. Because she could admit that she was feeling punchy and wasn't totally processing everything. God, it had happened *so* fast. And if Weston hadn't been there for her... She held back a shudder.

The detective raised an eyebrow at Weston. "Ms. Martinez isn't a suspect, and since the media would be an absolute circus, we'd already planned to make arrangements to talk to her somewhere else."

"Good," he bit out.

The detective sighed, then looked at her again, his expression softening. "I'm glad you're okay. Tonight could have ended a lot worse." His expression said he'd seen worse and then some.

"How's Rodrigo?" No one had been able to tell her much other than he was in the hospital with a broken leg and some contusions. The reason her bodyguard hadn't been able to get to her in time is because he'd gone for her guitarist, Natalia, who was closer and had saved her from certain death.

"He's at Memorial and currently undergoing surgery for his leg. It sounds as if he's going to be okay though. He was really lucky." He cleared his throat. "Look, I know it's not my business but I suggest you don't visit him there right now. It'll be a media circus and will probably upset his family."

"You know his family?" The way he'd said the last part made her think that he might.

"He used to work for the PD and my wife is friends with his sister-in-law."

"I hadn't actually planned to go for that very reason. Trust me, I know what kind of baggage I bring. Whatever medical bills his company's insurance doesn't cover, I'll be taking care of." She wasn't even sure why she was telling this detective. Okay, *lies*, it was because of guilt. She felt guilty that this freak thing had happened at her concert.

It was so hard to believe it was intentional—it had to be an accident. But either way, this was on her at the end of the day and she'd take responsibility for it.

The detective's eyebrows rose slightly but he nodded, then looked at Weston, his expression going hard again. Maybe the way they were reacting to each other was like some guy thing. "I suggest taking the south exit. The media seems to be convening at the main entrance and the west side. I'll leak it that you're leaving through the west side."

"Thanks." Weston nodded, waited for the detective to leave before he turned back to her. "Is there anything you need before we leave?"

"I mean... no. But I need to talk to Paige and my crew and—"

"Nope. You're going home. The faster everyone gets out of here, the better. This is an active crime scene—"

"We don't know that what happened was intentional."

His expression was dry, but he didn't argue. Instead he said, "We're leaving in two minutes. Your agent and anyone else you need can come to you. I'm taking you home now."

"What about the people you came with?" Rebel wasn't sure what was wrong with her, why she was pushing him on this. But she felt like a mess right now.

"They're all grownups and will get home on their own. Let's go."

"I've never seen you so bossy," she grumbled, picking up her bag and making sure it had everything she needed. Then she picked up the vase of flowers he'd brought her.

"Just leave those. Paige will make sure they make it home." His tone softened somewhat as he gently took it from her hands. "You've been through a lot and you're going to be crashing soon. You need to be home, to rest, when that happens. There's nothing else you can do tonight."

"Okay." She already felt the energy draining from her, knew he was right. She was going to send flowers to Rodrigo in the morning and everyone else was unharmed, if shaken up, so there really wasn't much she could do at this point. And if she was being honest, she wanted to be home, away from everyone and everything.

Well, everyone but Weston.

***

Rebel could barely keep her eyes open as she leaned back on the barstool at her kitchen island. Detective Duarte had shown up not long after Paige and Anna, so now the four of them plus Weston—who hadn't left her side—were hopefully about to wrap up. Because she was one hundred percent done processing anything else today.

"Thank you for stopping by and updating Rebel in person," Weston said as he stepped forward, held a hand out for the detective. Then in the smoothest, most polite shutdown she'd ever seen, he continued, "I'll walk you out to your vehicle. I've got a couple questions anyway."

Rebel blinked as the two of them headed out but was immediately pulled into a surprise hug from Anna. "I'm so glad you're okay."

"Thank you." She awkwardly patted Anna's back, the display of affection taking her off guard.

She'd made the mistake of getting too close to her first assistant and it had blown up in her face when some private photos had been released. Nothing horrible, but it had taken a toll on her mental health and had been a good lesson that she needed to keep her work and personal life separate.

Anna wiped at her face, swiping away some tears as she nodded. "Everything happened so fast."

"Yeah, I know. How are you doing?" Rebel had asked her earlier but wanted to check in anyway. "Do you need any time off?"

"Oh, no, I'm still a little flustered but I'm okay."

"We're all good," Paige added, clearly wanting to change subjects.

Rebel swore nothing fazed the woman.

"What do you think we should do?" she asked Paige, even though exhaustion was pulling her under. "About tomorrow night," she added. Though technically it was today, since it was now one in the morning. The cops weren't convinced it was intentional but were concerned that some of the security feeds had been compromised. They weren't certain if it had been sabotage or just a glitch brought on by a bunch of lingo she didn't totally understand. But combined with all the creepy letters she'd received lately—including death threats—they were taking the whole thing very seriously.

Paige was silent for a long moment, which was unlike her. "Honestly, I don't know. If the PD thinks it was intentional..." She scrubbed both hands over her face and dropped them. "It could be a nightmare if something else goes wrong."

"Should we cancel? I don't want anyone else getting hurt." Not that the cops were convinced it was on purpose, but still. She hated that they might have to cancel two shows though, considering the amount of money everyone would lose, including the venue.

"Red Stone Security has agreed to do a full sweep of the concert venue and add extra layers of security that have been lacking thus far, to the entire show. Tonight and for Sunday night," Weston said as he stepped back into the kitchen. Somehow he didn't look tired at all. If anything, he seemed keyed up and ready to take down any potential threats. "Nothing was damaged that can't be fixed immediately."

She wasn't sure how he was so alert right now, but it was insanely hot. And she really wanted to be alone with him. She'd been thinking about that almost kiss, wanted to know whether she'd imagined it or not.

"Really?" Paige turned to him, her expression speculative. "I think that would keep us safe from any potential litigious issues, if so. Let me talk to our lawyers and I'll get back to you. In the meantime," she said, turning to Rebel. "Get some rest. I'm going to cancel your interviews and the other engagement you've got tomorrow. So—"

"No." She shook her head. "Just move the engagement back an hour and let the interviewers know that their time is cut short by five minutes each. It'll be enough to make up for the time lost on the other thing. And I'm not canceling, so don't even."

Paige sighed, but nodded and pulled her into a brief hug, air kissing her on the cheek. "I'll see you in the morning then. Come on," she ordered Anna before ushering Rebel's assistant out.

Now that it was just her and Weston, Rebel felt as if she could breathe again, even as her internal nervousness keyed up. They'd almost kissed before the concert and while that shouldn't even matter now, the memory was fully embedded in her brain and wasn't going anywhere. "What do you think?"

"Hold on." He picked up the tablet on the countertop and set the security system to arm. He had her code, and had told her that he'd be taking over her security for the night and foreseeable future. She watched as he pulled up the cameras and set the tablet upright so he could keep an eye on things. "Okay. What's your engagement tomorrow?"

"Ah, I'm a special guest at a pet adoption tomorrow. The shelter is hoping to bring in more people."

"That sounds like a security nightmare." Weston looked absolutely horrified by the thought of her going.

"I committed months ago. It's the shelter Molly and Tag own." Friends from their old neighborhood. She was also planning on adopting a dog in the next couple weeks, once she got settled back in Miami. She'd wanted to for ages but not until she knew she'd be in one place for a while.

He blinked and she knew she'd won. "Damn it," he muttered.

Oh, she'd definitely won. "I can't cancel on the nicest humans I know," she added, to make sure it stuck. Molly and Tag had four kids and ran a pet shelter together, taking in animals from kill shelters that would have been put down otherwise.

"Fine. But I'm going, and your new security detail is too."

"I'm not arguing on having security, but it's really last-minute."

"I talked to one of the owners of Red Stone already," he said. "He's got a team ready to go and they'll be here at sunrise."

"Well thank you then. You know you don't have to go. I know you've got work and—"

His ice-blue eyes narrowed slightly. "Seriously? I almost lost you tonight. I'm not letting you out of my sight for the foreseeable future."

Ooohhh. Butterflies launched inside her at his tone. Combined with that maybe-almost-kiss earlier, and almost *dying*, her emotions were all over the place right now. Especially with his whole take-charge attitude. "Ah, are you sure Elliana is okay with that? And Van?" she tacked on.

"Yeah, they're fine." He glanced at the security feed, frowned as he scanned the cameras. "We've brought on some new people at the company and they'll live without me. Besides, if you hire Red Stone full time, I'll be a hero," he muttered.

She snorted as she slid off the stool. "Seriously?"

"Yep. Everyone there is a fan and Elliana is sort of obsessed with you." He ran a hand over his face and for the first time she saw how tired he was. Whatever mask he'd been wearing had slipped. "Though I'm not supposed to say anything."

"Oh." She wasn't sure how to take that. "Did you two ever date?" Did that sound as casual as she hoped? At this point, Rebel felt punch drunk and wasn't sure of anything.

He blinked in surprise, then snorted out a disbelieving laugh. "No. Hell no." Then he laughed even harder, his whole body shaking as if the very concept was ludicrous.

"Why is that funny? She's gorgeous."

"Yeah, I guess, but she's also a terrifying weapons expert. God, I can't imagine any man brave enough to date that maniac." He continued snickering slightly.

Relief punched through her harder than anything and she knew exactly why. He hadn't dated Elliana. Didn't mean he wasn't dating other people, but... that little jealous monster that had been riding her for months disappeared.

"I need a shower and sleep." She still had all her stage makeup on and even though Weston had given her a hoodie to wear, she had one of her dresses on underneath and wanted to get out of all this junk.

He sobered immediately. "Of course. I'll do a perimeter walk of your place and crash in one of your guest rooms."

Her instinct was to tell him that he didn't need to stay but she didn't want to be alone tonight. And having him so close by would go a long way in easing the fear that had taken root inside her that tonight's accident hadn't been an accident at all.

# CHAPTER 11

"Come in," Rebel called out.

Weston opened her bedroom door, stepping into the doorway. "Hey. House is secure, so you can sleep easy."

Rebel was sitting on the end of her bed wrapped in a bright pink fluffy robe, her damp hair braided and a remote control in her hand. But the television wasn't on. The blinds were up on the oversized windows that faced her back patio and pool. Everything in her backyard was lit up as if ready for a party, but her room was dim except for one lamp on her nightstand. The space was vast with a huge bed, two nightstands and a little sitting area by the window.

"Thank you," she murmured, looking lost and beyond exhausted. And for some reason she looked smaller than normal sitting there in the quiet. As if she might come apart at any second.

He should go. Even told himself to. But he didn't listen. Because he couldn't leave her looking so damn fragile. Tablet in hand, he took a couple steps into her inner sanctum, a place he'd never been. He'd imagined himself in her bedroom before but not like this. "You want some company for a bit? Maybe watch a movie?" Her eyelids were drooping but he realized she didn't want to be alone, could see it in the tense lines of her body. So he could pretend that he wanted to watch a movie.

The tension in her shoulders eased slightly. "Sure. If you want. You can pick." She tossed the remote down and scrambled back to the head of the bed to prop herself up against a bundle of pillows. She'd been like that even as a kid, with so many extra pillows that her bed ended up being half pillows. Though this was a California king, so they didn't completely cover the bed like with her twin bed from all those years ago. As she settled in, she picked up a small remote control on her nightstand and closed the blinds over the windows.

Weston picked up the television remote as he headed to the other side of the bed but didn't bother turning it on. "You're too tired for TV," he murmured, easing in beside her, wishing things were different between them. He couldn't even pretend to scroll through anything. She needed rest, though if she decided she wanted to get naked with him, then he was all in. They'd had a moment back in her dressing room, but then everything had gone to hell. And he certainly wasn't going to pressure her for anything or even bring up that sort-of almost kiss. Even if his dick had other ideas.

She sighed as she slid down slightly and he pulled the covers over her. "I know but I don't want to be alone." Her voice was quiet.

"I'm not going anywhere," he murmured. He needed a shower and a change of clothes but didn't give a shit. Not now. Not when she needed him. After the night she'd had and the likely fallout from it on the news, he wanted to be who she counted on. No matter what happened between them romantically. She'd been there for him when he'd been overseas, a lifeline he hadn't even realized he'd needed. But when she once missed emailing him for a few days in a row, it had hit him how much he'd depended on those messages from her. How much he loved her.

"Promise?" Her voice was drowsy as she closed her eyes, and he slid down slightly, propping two pillows beneath him.

He glanced at the tablet with the multiple camera feeds on the nightstand. "Always."

Closing his eyes, he tried to rest as she started to doze next to him. It was no wonder she was so damn tired, after everything that had happened. But he couldn't shut his mind off, not after tonight.

Once he was certain she was asleep, he slid from bed and grabbed his phone, shooting off a text to both Van and Elliana. They were likely still awake since they were both night owls. Then he texted Paige, hoping it wasn't too late. Though he doubted it, since Rebel's agent didn't seem to sleep.

Paige got back to him quicker than the others, sending him the link to a shared folder with all the nasty messages Rebel had received in the last six months. Because Weston was going to be taking an active role in her security now, whether she approved of it or not.

Tablet and phone with him, he slid back into Rebel's bed, glad when she didn't stir. But he couldn't resist pushing back some of her hair from her face.

She sighed, her expression so soft and relaxed it twisted him up inside. For the briefest moment he allowed himself to imagine what it would be like to be in her bed for real with her. Not just as her friend.

When his phone buzzed, he dropped his hand and glanced at the screen, surprised to see it was Anthony. He'd caught a ride with the man to the concert but had obviously gone home with Rebel after the shitshow.

*How's my girl?*

*She's not your girl,* he responded, then winced. Yeah, he probably *did* need some sleep.

To his surprise, Anthony responded with laughing emojis. Then, *You've got it bad.*

Weston decided not to be a total dick and responded. *She's asleep. Finally crashed.*

*Do the police know anything? Because I guarantee tonight wasn't an accident.*

*Why are you so sure?* Weston texted back. The police weren't sure of anything at this point.

*Because her people are incredibly thorough. I can't believe that what happened was an accident with all the checks they do.*

Weston agreed. Feeling surly, he texted back, *She needs more security.* Maybe if Rebel heard it from enough people close to her, she'd listen. Though at least starting tomorrow, Red Stone was going to be heading things up.

*No shit. But if you're going for it with her, then you better get used to having security around and her lifestyle. Because if you can't handle it, walk away now before you break her heart.*

Weston sat back against the headboard, looked over at Rebel. Walk away? Hell no. Never. *I can handle anything.* At least for Rebel. He'd take on the entire world for her. He was surprised Anthony seemed to understand his feelings for her. Weston thought he'd been good at burying everything.

*That's what everyone says until shit gets real.*

Weston paused, wondered if this was about something else. *Is everything okay with you and Bailey?*

*Yes! But he's the exception to the rule. And I love Rebel so if you hurt her, I'll hurt you.*

*You shouldn't put threats in text format, for future reference.*

He got more laughing emojis. Then, *I knew I liked you for a reason. Keep me updated because Rebel likes to pretend that everything is fine. I want details.*

*I promise.*

He got a thumbs up back so he set his phone down, then logged into the folder of messages Paige had sent him. And wanted to puke as he read over some of them.

*You looked like a whore onstage.*

*Have you gained weight? You looked like a cow at your last concert.*

*What happened to you? You used to sing with heart, now you just sound like a stupid whore.*

Something was seriously wrong with people, he thought. Instead of focusing on all of the hate, he added all the messages to a program Van had created to look for various similarities and syntax, and let it run in the background as he started typing up a security plan for Rebel.

Because he'd made a decision. She was his, and even if she decided that they'd only ever be friends—something he refused to believe, considering they'd almost kissed before her concert—he was going to do everything to make sure she was as safe as humanly possible. And not just this weekend, but it was a good start.

She was always taking care of everyone else. Someone needed to take care of her, and it was damn sure going to be him.

# CHAPTER 12

Showered and feeling more centered, Rebel stepped into her kitchen to find Weston making breakfast and her coffee pot already brewed. She'd woken up alone and had tried to push down the punch of disappointment, but now she understood why he'd left.

"Hey," she murmured, feeling a little self-conscious in a way she'd never been with him. In the past she'd have never cared about being in her robe with her hair wrapped up in a towel, but things felt very different now. As if they'd crossed an invisible line with him staying in her bed. And... that almost kiss. Which she'd been obsessing about nonstop.

She'd fallen asleep with Weston next to her and while nothing had remotely happened, something had shifted between them. Though if she was being honest, things had shifted a long time ago, at least for her.

But the little girl inside of her was terrified that if things went wrong between her and Weston, if he saw right through to the core of her, that he'd find her wanting and walk away. She traveled a lot, had a stressful job, could be very demanding, had actual photographers stalking her half the time—not prime girlfriend or relationship material.

She just needed to forget about that almost kiss and they could go back to normal. Yep. That was the sane thing to do.

"Hey yourself," Weston murmured, looking up from the stove. "How'd you sleep?"

"Surprisingly well." Especially considering it was only seven o'clock. But she'd slept so hard and the shower had felt amazing. And now that she'd gotten real sleep, she was able to process the incident from yesterday more clearly. As long as they beefed up their security and did a thorough check of everything then they should be fine to keep both shows going. "What about you?"

"I'm good, and I hope you're hungry."

Her stomach growled and she laughed lightly. "I think that answers your question. Listen, Weston, you don't need to be doing all this for me. I know you have a job and other responsibilities." She'd been taking care of herself for a long time.

"You're not a responsibility. You're one of my oldest friends and lucky for me, I make my own hours. So I'm not going anywhere." His tone was so matter-of-fact as he plated her spinach, pepper, and mushroom omelet—exactly what she'd been craving. "You need to eat and get ready because the Red Stone people will be here soon. Van already dropped off a bag of clothes for me, so I'm going to use one of your guest showers."

She blinked as he slid the plate in front of her, then started pouring her a mug of coffee. A thread of panic slid through her, creeping right into all the little crevices that told her this was so bad.

So very bad. Because she could get used to him being around all the time, start to crave it. Depend on it. On him. And that was a little scary.

"Weston, I..." She trailed off as he set the mug in front of her, then leaned down—and holy shit, brushed his lips over hers.

Just totally kissed her. It was the barest hint of a touch, his gorgeous lips skating over hers as if this had happened a hundred times before. Then he nipped her bottom lip and pulled back, heat simmering in his blue eyes.

She blinked. Opened her mouth, then shut it again as heat slid through her, warming her up from the inside out. Until yesterday, she'd only allowed herself to fantasize about Weston, but not in a real way. Her fantasies had always been more about sex, but with him in her space, taking care of her, they were taking on a mind of their own. Especially after that little kiss. Oh, she was in soooo much trouble. That was definitely not enough for her.

"Eat. I'll be back."

"My life is complicated," she blurted when he took a step away from her. Seriously, what was he thinking? Why did he want her? She needed to give him a head's up that her life was a lot to deal with.

Now he was the one to blink. "What?"

"Whatever this is," she said, motioning between them. "Whatever is happening, I don't think it's a good idea, Weston. I've got too much going on." *Lies. It's a great idea*, her inner voice said.

But he'd eventually get sick of all the craziness of her life. Of the paparazzi following her around, speculating on every little thing, right down to why she chose to wear a black dress instead of a pink one. As if there was some secret meaning behind it. No one wanted that, and especially not someone like Weston who valued his privacy. He'd built up a company based on giving people online privacy. He'd get sick of it, and her eventually, and then he'd break her heart. Either because he stayed out of a sense of obligation or he'd leave her. And he was the one constant in her life.

"I think it's the best damn idea I've had in a long time," he growled. "Now eat before I take you right on this countertop."

Um, what did he just say? Heat punched through her as he stalked off, and all she could do was stare at his perfect ass as she tried to digest his words. What the hell had just happened?

***

"This is today's schedule. You should have already received it from your boss, but I want to go over a few things," Weston said to the Red Stone Security employees, Juan and Nash.

"We got the schedule," Juan murmured, looking around Rebel's expansive kitchen before focusing back on Weston. "And we'd like to do a perimeter check as well."

Weston nodded. "You will but not this morning. She's got a social thing soon, then a bunch of interviews back-to-back. And I don't care what her agent says or what any of the interviewers try to say, one of you is with her at all times. Period. She's not to be alone with anyone."

Both men nodded. "Absolutely," Nash added. "We've guarded celebrities before and understand how stupid people can get around them. I think it's why we were chosen for this assignment."

Weston knew that already, since he'd handpicked them. He'd looked over their resumes, which were both impressive considering neither of them had been with the company that long. But he liked what he saw. Both had military experience, a handful of medals each, were both financially solid, happily married (yeah, he'd checked) and as they'd said, had guarded a number of celebrities in Miami. "I chose you two based on your resumes and the feedback you both received from clients." That had been the tipping point. People loved these two and couldn't sing their praises enough.

They both looked faintly surprised, then Juan said, "I've been hearing a lot of buzz about your company's new app. It's a game changer with security."

He half smiled. "That's the hope." He and his team had been working on something that would revolutionize privacy and eliminate a good portion of data mining everyone experienced. "Do you have any questions for me?"

"Not right now, no, but we do need access to the location app for Ms. Martinez," Juan said.

"You can call me Rebel, please," Rebel said as she strode into the kitchen, dressed casually in jeans, bright purple sneakers and a T-shirt that said 'Dogs Make Me Happy'. And when she turned her megawatt smile on, Weston felt the punch of it right to his core. She had large sunglasses on the top of her head, her dark hair pulled back into a sleek ponytail and simple gold hoop earrings.

Both men straightened slightly at her entrance, but neither gave her that starstruck look he'd witnessed countless times from others. They were definitely off to a good start.

"I've got food and coffee if you're hungry, but if not, I'm ready to go." She looked at Weston and her carefully constructed mask was in place.

As if they hadn't kissed earlier. Though it had barely been a kiss, just a brushing of lips. But he'd wanted her to know where he stood. She was skittish, but that was okay. He'd known her a long time; he wasn't going anywhere, but he had a feeling it was going to take time for him to convince her of that.

Everyone in her family had abandoned her, including her mom. Though her mother had died a few years ago, before Rebel really made it, she'd been asking for money from Rebel even then. Harassing her and begging for help with rent or whatever. The list of her mom's "needs" had been endless. And Rebel had usually caved, sending her money.

"I'm not hungry," Weston murmured. Not for food anyway.

The others replied with the same so they headed out, with Nash driving Red Stone's SUV and Juan sitting in the back with Rebel. Weston wanted to sit on the other side of her, but her body language was tense. So even if he wanted to push her some, now wasn't the time. She was about to get photographed by hundreds of people probably and would want to feel at ease and in charge. Not worrying about him.

"So you like Angel's Bakery?" Juan asked Rebel.

Nash cleared his throat, but Juan ignored him.

"Uh, yeah, it's amazing. How do you know that?" Rebel asked.

"My wife owns it and said you tagged her shop the other day." His tone said he was proud of his wife, which were some points for him.

Weston really liked what these two seemed to bring to the table, but there was only so much he could decide based on their resumes. Which was why he planned on being with her all day. He wanted to get a feel for how they were in person.

"Oh my gosh, that place is amazing. If I lived closer I'd eat there all the time."

"It's hard not to eat there all the time," he said, laughing. "So are you excited about the show tonight?"

It was obvious to Weston that Juan was making an effort to put her at ease, that his friendliness was natural. It went along with some of the comments former principals had said about him; that he was authentic and friendly while still doing his job. This was likely the reason Juan was the one sitting in the back and Nash was driving.

"Ah, yeah, if it's still happening. My agent and I have been texting this morning and she seems to think it's still a go."

"From what I heard it's still happening. Red Stone has a whole crew working with the stadium now to do a thorough security check."

He tuned out their conversation and glanced at Nash, who was alert, scanning around them as he drove.

"So your wife owns a pet shelter, right?" Weston asked Nash quietly.

Nash shot him a surprised look.

"I looked into both of you thoroughly." And he wasn't sorry about it. Might as well be up front.

Nash snorted softly. "I don't blame you. People are crazy," he murmured as he turned on his signal, switched lanes. "And yeah, she owns one but doesn't work there day to day. My wife is thrilled about what Rebel is doing today, though. She knows the owners of the shelter and said they take on the most pitiful pets that are the least likely to get adopted."

Yeah, that sounded about right. Weston hadn't seen Molly or Tag in years, but Molly had been taking care of stray animals from the time she was eight. He'd done a search of both of them last night as well, digging into their financials and a few other things, and they seemed to still be the kind people he remembered. They hadn't made it to Aunt Margaret's funeral, but they'd sent flowers and a card.

Weston started to respond but his phone buzzed in his pocket. "Excuse me," he murmured and began returning the multitude of texts that seemed to come in all around the same time. A couple from Detective Duarte, some from Paige, and then work stuff that he back-burnered for now.

By the time he was done, Nash had parked behind the pet shelter as Weston had previously instructed.

The plan was for Rebel to put in some face time, take some pictures, then quietly leave out the back. Only then would the shelter and Rebel be posting about it on social media, hoping to pull more people to the place. If she'd posted about it beforehand, the place would be an absolute madhouse with people rushing to see her, not the animals.

He loved that she'd put so much thought into this. Well... he loved everything about the complicated woman.

# CHAPTER 13

Rebel sat on her knees, trying to remain as still as possible as Jupiter, the older dog of undetermined origin—maybe part border collie? — eyed her from across his room at the pet shelter. He seemed almost hunched in on himself as he watched her closely. She knew from Molly that Jupiter was roughly ten years old, about forty-five pounds and came from a hoarding situation, so he was nervous about everything and everyone, except a Chihuahua who was his best friend.

He was one of their longest residents, along with Lucky, the yippy little Chihuahua. Jupiter was brown and white, with one ear that pointed up while the other seemed to do what it wanted.

"Hello, sweet boy," she murmured. "You want pets?" She'd been stalking Molly's website, where she posted pictures of incoming dogs looking for good homes, and had somehow missed this guy until recently. As soon as she'd seen him and read his story, she'd fallen in love.

She felt Molly step into the room behind her before her friend spoke. "This one is going to need a lot of love. And he won't leave without Lucky. I think it would be cruel to separate them."

Lucky had one ear and a yippy bark and he'd jumped eagerly into Rebel's arms about twenty minutes ago. Then he'd promptly peed on her. "Lucky is a tiny terror," Rebel murmured on a laugh, glad that she was getting some private time with Jupiter while Lucky was off taking care of business outside.

Molly sat next to her, huffing out a laugh. "You're not wrong. But they both deserve to be homed together. I understand you wanted a dog, not *dogs*, so trust me when I say I'm not judging if you decide to keep looking. We have plenty of older dogs here who need good homes."

Rebel glanced at her longtime friend, who was pregnant again, her hand resting on her baby bump as she made soft little sounds to Jupiter.

Who was scooting slowly toward them, dragging his legs behind him even though she knew he could walk. "What's he doing?"

"He always does this when he's nervous—so most of the time and especially with strangers."

Jupiter finally made his way over to the two of them and set his head on Molly's lap, but turned his face toward Rebel, his expression curious.

"Lean your head on my shoulder slowly. Let him see how much I like you."

Rebel did just that, laying her head on Molly's shoulder. "You are the sweetest pup I've ever seen," she whispered to Jupiter.

Both his ears stood up at that and he moved his head a little closer to Rebel, his black nose almost touching her knee. But not quite. Then he started thumping his tail against the concrete in a rapid rhythm as he looked up at her with those big eyes.

"Can I pet him or is it too soon?"

"He's never wagged his tail like this with someone new, so I think you should try."

"Probably just smells Lucky's pee all over me," she muttered, but couldn't stop her smile as she slowly reached out and scratched the top of his head.

His tongue lolled out and his tail went wild as she scritched behind his ears.

"Oh, I think you're mine," she murmured. This sweet boy had been abandoned by everyone. Yeah, he was coming home with her for sure.

"He's a big responsibility." Molly's voice was kind, but hesitant.

"I know. And I'll be taking Lucky too. Not today, but next Friday if that's okay with you." She'd already pre-filled all the paperwork ahead of time and had been thinking about adopting a dog for over a year. Once she was done with her last couple shows, she had a few things to wrap up and then could get her place ready for two dogs.

"Rebel, I appreciate you coming today, but—"

"Why are you trying to talk me out of this? Do *you* want to take him home? Because it's okay if you do. I can keep looking." She really hoped that wasn't the case because the way Jupiter was looking up at her, it was clear he had so much love to give.

"What? No. I mean, yes, if I could. I actually tried but Lucky kept getting into fights with my gentle old German shepherd. I even tried separating Jupiter and Lucky, but they were both depressed so I had to put them back together. I just... I love these two. They've been adopted twice before but it didn't work out. I'm just worried, that's all."

Oh, well that she could understand. "I've been thinking about this for over a year. This has always been something I planned to do. My house has enough room for them, and I can literally bring them with me to work if I want. I'm currently having a recording studio built on the back side of my property too so... these two are probably going to be sick of me because I'm never going to leave them alone. I've done a lot of research and plan to be with them nonstop for the first few weeks as we all get used to each other and get into a rhythm. This isn't a whim. I'm going to build their trust and I won't break it. Once I bring them home, that's it."

"I wish everyone was like you," Molly said, then cursed herself when a few tears escaped. "Sorry, this pregnancy has made my hormones go nuts." She looked down at Jupiter, who was now nuzzling her gently. "I'm going to miss this baby."

"I promise to send you pictures and updates of both of them."

"I know you will. And thank you for coming down today. I can't tell you what a difference this is going to make. The last time you came by, we ended up having almost all of our animals adopted out—and by really good people. They still send pictures and updates to us."

"It's no problem. I love this, and thank you for the shirt by the way. I'd really like to pay for it though." She motioned to the hot pink T-shirt with the shelter's logo on it. "Seriously."

"Are you kidding me? Lucky peed on you! Besides, if you do a video with that shirt on or wear it to your interviews, it's the best marketing in the world. I'll give you all the shirts if you want," she said, her grin cheeky.

"I'll definitely wear it to my interviews today then."

"You are the best."

Jupiter had moved his head back to Rebel's lap and she was soaking it up, practically preening that he was letting her get so close, so soon. Unlike Lucky, she thought. That one was going to be a tougher nut to crack, but that was okay. She had enough love for both of them. "True." Rebel grinned.

"So... what's up with you and Weston?"

Against her will, Rebel felt her cheeks warm. "Ah, what do you mean?"

Molly blinked as she looked at her. "I hope no one who interviews you today asks about him because you've got the worst poker face. I swear to god, you two need to just bang it out and get married."

"Molly!" Married? What the hell!

She shrugged. "Once Tag finally pulled his head out of his ass and banged *me*, everything was good in the world."

"I'm not having this conversation, and I can't believe sweet Molly O'Hare is talking about *banging*."

Molly just grinned. "I've got four kids and one on the way, the jig is up, I bang all the time," she said around a laugh. Then she shifted her legs slightly as she started to stand.

Jupiter raced away from them, running back to his fluffy dog bed, his tail tucked hard between his legs as he stared at Rebel.

Her heart melted. Poor little one. She was going to give him and Lucky the best home. "I'm coming back for you. And your little sister too. Just you wait."

Jupiter simply continued to watch her with those big cartoon eyes. She couldn't imagine how anyone could bring him back. Ugh. People sucked, something she knew more than most.

As she stood, she dusted some of the dog fur off her jeans, and as she and Molly headed out of the kennel, Tag was walking down the hallway toward them, Lucky yipping in his arms. The man was massive, bigger and taller than Weston, and he only had eyes for Molly. Always had.

"So? What's the verdict?" he asked, setting Lucky down.

The little Chihuahua raced up to her, her nails clicking on the concrete. She barked out something excitedly to Rebel, then ran in to join Jupiter, jumping into the bed with him and cuddling up close. Jupiter laid his head protectively over her as she curled into him.

"Apparently I only need one bed for them. Or maybe like one bed for each room so they always have their own spot." Because she was going to spoil the hell out of them.

Molly let out a startled laugh as she slid an arm around her husband's waist. "I hope you do just that. They deserve it."

Even the reserved Tag grinned and nodded. "You should start an Insta account for them."

She blinked up at him. "I didn't even think you were on social media."

"I'm not, but Molly is and I like looking at the animal accounts." He lifted a big shoulder. "And you need to find Weston. The man is practically foaming at the mouth waiting for you."

Ooohhhh. Heat curled between her legs at the thought that Weston was impatient to see her. Because god knew she wanted to be close to him. Especially after that sorta-kiss from only a couple hours ago.

How was it only a couple hours? It was like he'd lured her in with that little kiss and now all she could think about was kissing him again, but deeper, harder and maybe without their clothes on. It didn't matter that it was a bad idea. She couldn't turn off her attraction to him.

She mostly ignored the 'foaming at the mouth' comment and hugged them both before waving to her soon-to-be new dogs. Nash, Juan and Weston were all waiting for her at the end of the hallway, but she only had eyes for Weston.

Even the sound of barking and yipping dogs faded as she got lost in his blue eyes.

"Did you make a decision?" he asked.

"Yep." She couldn't contain her grin. "I'm picking them up next Friday."

"Them?"

"Two dogs. They're a package deal and I couldn't separate them. They're absolutely adorable." Well, one was going to be tough but that was alright.

Weston gave her the softest smile, then slid an arm around her shoulders as they stepped out of the hallway and headed for the back door of the shelter. She'd already taken pictures with people out front and as soon as they were in the SUV, she was going to do another quick live video promoting the adoption event. She'd already done one in the kennel before showing some of the dogs but she wanted to do another one.

Rebel leaned into Weston, trying not to obsess over the feel of his arm protectively around her. Because it felt so damn right.

"Paparazzi across the street," Juan murmured as he held open the back door of the vehicle for Rebel.

She didn't bother looking in that direction as she slid in and buckled her seatbelt. But she did wonder if it annoyed Weston. It was simply part of her life now, though she knew once she settled back into Miami it would ease off for a while at least.

To her surprise, her two bodyguards sat up front and Weston sat next to her.

"Is everything okay?" She kept her voice down but the other two could hear no matter what. She was brimming with excitement and wanted to talk about Jupiter and Lucky but something was going on with him, she could sense it.

"Yeah." His gaze fell to her mouth for an instant, then he cleared his throat.

"No it's not. What's wrong? Did you talk to the detective?" Something was off.

"No." He paused, seemed to weigh something, then shoved out a breath. "I ran some of the messages and letters you received through a program Van made, and a handful are definitely from the same creep. I was reading over them and…" He lifted his shoulder, but the action was jerky. "I hate people sometimes, that's all."

Ah, that was what this was about. She rested her hand lightly on his knee. "I know, but the good outweigh the bad. Or at least that's what I tell myself."

He looked at her mouth again, and she could almost swear he was going to kiss her. He definitely wanted to.

Aaaaand, she would kiss him back. Rebel felt like a mess right now, and deep down she just knew that things between them could explode once her lifestyle got to be too much for him, but she desperately wanted to take the chance anyway.

Wanted to throw caution to the wind, grab onto him and never let go. He was worth the risk even if she was terrified of getting burned at the end.

But then he cleared his throat and sat back, pulling up his phone. "We're a little early for your interviews so you've got time to do that feed about the pet shelter."

As disappointment sliced through her, she sat back and pulled out her own phone. Even if she wanted to dwell on it, it was good he didn't kiss her, at least here and now. What was she going to do, have a make-out session in front of her new bodyguards? God, she needed to keep her head on straight. At least Weston was thinking clearly. "I can't believe Paige let you take over everything so easily."

"She didn't have a choice," he murmured, his tone as hard as his expression. "And I'm not messing with anything she does. I'm simply tightening up your security."

Rebel wasn't sure what it said about her, but hoooooly hotness, heat punched through her at his commanding tone. Her entire body warmed up as she thought of him taking charge in other ways, namely when they were naked.

Then she ordered her inner voice to shut the hell up because she couldn't be walking around the rest of the day all flustered and flushed and aroused.

Taking a deep breath, she focused on what she planned to say for her video, rehearsed it in her head, then held her phone up to make a quick clip. It was easy to be excited because she truly was. This shelter mattered and she was so excited to finally be getting her own dog—dogs. As she spoke, she made sure to get a shot of her T-shirt as well and when she was done, she realized Juan was looking at her from the front seat. "What?"

"I can't believe you just did that spur of the moment. You almost convinced me to get a dog too. I bet that whole shelter gets cleared out today."

"I hope so." Well, except for her two dogs. Those angels were coming home with her soon.

"Me too. I'll find out later when I meet up with Tag," Juan continued.

"You're friends with Tag?" She was surprised since they hadn't seemed to know each other.

Juan shrugged. "Just met him, but we exchanged numbers. Angel and I are going to get together with him and his wife next week sometime. He might just want to convince me to adopt a dog but I don't care. That guy's alright."

Nash just shook his head, but she saw his amused expression in the rearview mirror. "He makes friends everywhere we go," he murmured.

Juan just rolled his eyes, then said, "Oh, Tag said to tell you that they'll take care of your shirt and get it back to you. I figured you didn't want a shirt that smells like dog pee just cooking in the SUV all day anyway."

She giggled lightly and wondered if she could ask about getting Juan and Nash as her full-time bodyguards, at least while she was in Miami. They took their jobs seriously, but they were so easy to be around. Mainly Juan, but it was clear they worked well together.

And Weston definitely liked them.

At that thought, she pulled out her phone and texted Weston, even though he was sitting right next to her. *You look hot today*, she said, knowing she was playing with fire. Who was she kidding? She was playing with a whole box of matches and a jug of kerosene. But she was feeling high from the shelter and the man of her actual dreams was sitting next to her looking gorgeous.

He glanced down at his phone, then stilled. But to give him credit he didn't look in her direction. Instead, he placed his big hand on her knee and oh so gently began massaging her inner leg. And she felt the touch all the way up her leg and to her core.

Fire indeed.

*Don't start teasing me now*, he typed.

*Who's teasing? I keep thinking about that kiss. I want more.*

He sucked in a short breath, then looked out the window and shifted slightly in his seat.

*Rebel...*

*Don't leave me in suspense.* She couldn't stop the grin from spreading across her face.

Weston scrubbed a hand over his face and looked at her, his expression heated. Then he texted again. *I'm tempted to take you right over my knee.*

Oh. Ooooh. She blinked as she reread his message. That should not get her so turned on but heat infused her as she typed back. *Don't make promises you can't keep.* She wasn't sure what had come over her but now that she knew he was in to her, she couldn't seem to stop herself. That little voice in the back of her head was still insistently telling her this was a mistake but maybe crashing and burning would be worth it if she got a taste of him.

He made a strangled sound and put his phone away.

She bit back another grin. They hadn't just crossed a line, they'd obliterated it. Just full on blew it up. Even as she worried that it might be a mistake, she couldn't find it in her to care as erotic images flooded her mind.

Well, fantasies. Ones she hoped they got to act out very, very soon.

# CHAPTER 14

Weston stood with Juan by the food and drinks table as Rebel sat across from yet another interviewer. This one was a local blogger and it was clear that Rebel knew and liked the woman asking her questions.

"She actually likes this one," Juan murmured next to him. "She's so nice to everyone but her smiles change slightly with people she doesn't care for."

"Yeah." He'd picked up on that too, but he'd seen Rebel's different faces over the years so it wasn't much of a surprise. The masks she wore with people to put on a happy face. She sure as hell hadn't been doing that with him in the SUV.

Maybe texting was easier for her to communicate. Whatever the hell had happened to shift things between them, he just wished they were back at her place or his place right now with no interruptions for hours. Days.

Hell, weeks.

He didn't want to get ahead of himself, but it was hard not to. And he had to resist the urge to pull out his phone again, to look at the messages. Not to mention he needed to stop thinking about them, because he had to be in control, now of all times. Rebel was his to protect.

He looked back at her, drank her in as she smiled at the woman talking to her. They'd arrived a little over an hour ago and Paige had been in a panic that Rebel wouldn't have time to get her makeup done and a bunch of other things. Of course there had been enough time, though.

He wasn't sure what they'd needed to do at all because Rebel was perfect as she was, but apparently she would 'look shiny' on camera without the proper makeup. There was a lot about her business he didn't know, and some he wasn't sure he'd ever understand, but at least the security he could handle. "I'll be back," he murmured to Juan when his phone buzzed in his pocket.

He stepped out of the room to find Nash standing guard and a short line of people waiting for their turn to do an interview. The setup for the interviews was simple and easy to keep her secure. No one went in the room that they didn't approve, period. Luckily Paige was in charge of vetting and had kept the list of people relatively short.

Not wanting to be overheard, he strode down the hallway in the opposite direction and answered. "Weston here."

"Hey," Detective Duarte said upon greeting. "I got the report back about last night and our forensics think it was intentional. The way the wires snapped, it was clear they'd been weakened previously. But they could have gone at any time during the show, so the actual timing wasn't perfected. It just happened to be near the end."

"Jesus," he muttered. "She's gotten a lot of threats over the years."

"Yeah, we know. Right now I'm running a facial recognition program over the video recordings from last night to see if we can match any faces with any of the letter senders."

He frowned. "I thought the security feeds were corrupted."

"The ones around the stage and private rooms were, but I'm talking about the recordings of the entire concert. All the people who entered and left and basically any videos taken from that night and earlier in the day. I'm planning to talk to any locals who sent her nasty messages first, but I'm hoping to get a lead with the facial recognition. If I can place someone who sent her threatening messages at the scene, or at least the vicinity, it'll be a hell of a lot easier to bring them in for questioning. And hopefully hold them."

Okay, so the handsome bastard was good at his job it seemed. "Good. What else? Rebel said she's a go for tonight and tomorrow."

"The crime scene has been cleared and I've talked to Grant Caldwell, one of the owners of Red Stone. They're taking this seriously and I trust him with my life. We're going to be adding cameras, however. In case whoever tampered with the wiring comes back."

"Good. She's in interviews now, and we've got two Red Stone employees with her at all times. What would you think if I did a dive on social media and pulled any public videos from the concert? If you add those to your search, you might get more hits."

"That's a huge undertaking," the detective said.

"Not as hard as you think." Not with the software his company had. Aaaand, he was going to call in a favor for this one, ask Elliana to help out.

"Good. Send me what you find. And I'll be in touch if I need anything." The detective disconnected before he could respond and Weston pocketed his phone.

As he did, the door closest to him opened up and Anna stepped out of a room with Lia. He didn't know Rebel's assistant well but her background check was clean and she seemed nice enough. Same with Lia, the woman who did the opening show for Rebel.

"I'm grabbing Rebel's tea now," Anna rushed out when she saw him. Lia didn't glance his way as she headed in the opposite direction, talking into her phone.

"Ah, okay." Why was she telling him this?

"I just didn't want you to think I was slacking." She wrung her hands in front of her, watching him nervously.

He frowned. He wasn't her boss. "Okay."

Anna raced off, her heels clacking along the hallway loudly.

What was that about? Maybe he would need to look deeper into her. He made a note of it as he made another phone call.

"Hey!" Elliana answered on the second ring. "How is she? How are you? What's going on? I saw her video at the pet shelter so obviously she's okay. But what the hell is going on?"

He'd talked to both Elliana and Van last night via text, but hadn't since then. Weston briefly brought her up to speed, then said, "You know how you have incredible computer skills?"

"Uh huh."

"And how you love me?"

"Oh my god, what do you want?"

"I told the detective that I could pull public videos from social media to add to his facial rec scan."

She snorted loudly. "*You're* gonna do that?"

"Come on. Do it for Rebel."

"Of course I will, but... I can pull more than public ones. Do you want everything?" She sounded a little gleeful now, and he knew why. In addition to blowing stuff up, she loved hacking.

"I figured that was unspoken. I don't care what you get or how you get it, just grab every feed possible. If one of those letter writers was at her concert, I want to know."

"If you want, I can try to hack into the PD's system and get updates for you."

Weston scrubbed a hand over his face. "That sounds..."

"Sounds like a yes. Okay I'll get to work, but you owe me."

"Seriously?"

"Nah. But I'm doing it for her, not you."

"Okay, I'm incredibly grateful, but why are you so obsessed with Rebel?" Weston knew why *he* was, but as far as he knew, Elliana was straight so it wasn't about that.

"Oh, because none of your goddamn business." She hung up on him.

As he pocketed his phone again, Anna raced back by him, a few different to-go cups in hand. He followed after her into the interview room to find Rebel alone with Juan.

"We're taking a five-minute break," she said when she saw him. Standing, she stretched and took the drink Anna offered her with a murmured thanks.

"Do you need longer?" he asked. Five minutes didn't seem like enough. Her entire day was packed with only a couple minute breaks here and there. Not that she seemed to mind, but he wanted to make sure she was taking care of herself.

Anna cleared her throat. "Well, Paige said—"

"I don't care what Paige says," Weston murmured, trying to keep his tone light and friendly enough. The younger woman was skittish as hell and he thought he might scare her.

"Five is good." Rebel grinned at him. "Promise. We only have like ten left I think, so with five to seven minutes each, we'll be out of here soon."

"Okay, well, I've got a few more things to handle before this afternoon," Anna said to Rebel. "I'll see you back at the house?"

"Sounds good." Rebel waited until Anna left and snickered. "I think you scared her!"

Juan snorted too.

"What?" Weston looked between the two of them. "I didn't do anything."

"I told you that your face is scary."

"My face is scary? Seriously?"

"I don't mean like that," she said, laughing even harder. "But I've never seen Anna like that. Maybe try smiling at her?"

He just shook his head and pulled his phone out, sent a text to Rebel. *Maybe later you sit on my face?*

Her eyes widened when she saw it, then her face flushed bright pink. She didn't even bother to text him back, just glared at him. "*Weston.*"

He just grinned and tucked his phone away, glad that Juan was choosing to ignore the two of them for the moment. Now that this door had opened with Rebel, there was no going back.

As Nash opened the door and let someone else in, Weston looked down at his buzzing phone again. A message from Elliana.

*I'm headed to your place, gonna set up shop there. Already got some hits, so stop by once Rebel is safe at her place. Or bring her if you want but you might not want her to see some of this shit. It's gross.*

Good mood fading, he texted her back a thumbs up and pocketed his phone again. Not only was he going to stake his claim with Rebel, he was going to end the threat to her permanently.

# CHAPTER 15

"I'm sorry to do this," Weston murmured to Rebel, who was leaning against her kitchen island top. "I'm leaving only because I need to, and because you're safe." Both Nash and Juan were in the house, as well as Paige, Anna and a couple other people involved in tonight's show. But they were giving him and Rebel privacy for a few minutes because he'd asked.

Or ordered. Whatever. He'd tried to smile while doing it.

"Weston, you have no reason to be sorry. I don't expect you to be with me twenty-four seven. You're not in charge of my security."

He snorted. Not yet he wasn't. But he'd taken on the role for now anyway and planned to make it a permanent thing. No one cared more about her safety than him.

She narrowed her eyes at him, but continued as she placed a gentle hand on his chest. "What happened last night is scary. Okay, terrifying. But it sounds like the police have things under control and we're doing everything we can to make sure tonight goes off without a hitch. I'm not leaving my house for a few hours anyway, so everything is okay."

He was able to breathe easier only because he knew she'd be staying put.

"What are you doing anyway?" she continued.

Damn it. He'd hoped she wouldn't ask because he didn't want to lie. "I'm not going to tell you because it will give you plausible deniability."

She blinked, but just as quickly her eyes narrowed. "Uh, so that means you're doing something illegal?" She grabbed onto his shirt and tugged him down close. "You better not be doing anything that can get you hurt or thrown in jail!"

"I promise." Mostly.

"I don't know if I believe you," she growled. "I mean, I'll bail you out, but you better not be doing something stupid."

The way she actually growled was adorable. "Rebel," he murmured, not sure what the hell he wanted to say. "I'm making sure you're safe," was what he settled on. Because he might do something stupid. For her, he'd do anything. "I'm not going to let anyone hurt you, Rebel! You could have been... anything could have happened to you last night. Those wires could have snapped at any time and I might not have been close enough to save you." He broke out in a sweat thinking about it.

Her expression softened. "I'm right here and I'm okay. I just need to know that you won't do anything where you might get hurt. I can't lose you either."

Oh hell. Seeing the concern on her expression and hearing it in her voice unraveled him. In response, he leaned down and kissed her, threading his fingers through her hair and cupping the back of her head as he claimed her mouth. He'd been thinking about this all day and wasn't going another moment without kissing her.

Groaning, she leaned into him immediately as he pinned her to the countertop. When she flicked her tongue against his, arching her body into his, he growled into her mouth, wishing he didn't have to go.

Wishing for a hell of a lot of things. This was the woman of his dreams, the woman no one else could compare to. And he was officially kissing her, tasting her, being consumed by her.

But his priority now was her, not his dick. And the faster he checked in with Elliana, the faster he could get back here. To Rebel.

With nothing but regret, he pulled away, loved the way her cheeks were flushed and her eyes were slightly dazed as she looked up at him. "I'll be thinking about you while I'm gone. And I'll be back as soon as possible, but I've got my phone on me so call or text if you need. I'll pick up no matter what." There was a hell of a lot more he wanted to say to her, but now wasn't the time.

"What are we doing?" she whispered, her expression raw and vulnerable for a flash of a moment.

"Something we should have been doing for a long time." He kissed her again, then pulled back when he heard heels clicking in a nearby hallway. "Call me if you need me."

It was clear she wanted to say more, but Paige, Anna and a couple others entered so she pasted on a smile for them. He used that time to escape, only stopping to briefly talk to Juan and Nash before he headed home.

Thankfully it only took a minute to get there. He was surprised to find another vehicle sitting next to Elliana's. One he didn't recognize. A bright teal Jeep with random stickers on the back.

Inside he found Elliana and... Lizzy Caldwell in his office. The space was huge and when he'd moved in, he'd designated half of it to be used for in-person meetings and online conference calls. With the way the world was changing, and with how much global business they were starting to do, it made sense to have a space at home for international calls or meetings. Right now he was glad for the privacy.

"Lizzy. Good to see you." He didn't keep the surprise out of his voice as he strode in and sat across from the two women, who had two laptops each set up in front of them. He knew her from the work his company had been doing with Red Stone, but she and Elliana worked together a lot more. And seemed to be friends too. Which made sense, since they were both essentially hackers. Though Elliana preferred to simply blow up her problems, she could metaphorically blow shit up too.

"Weston," Lizzy said with a nod, her fingers flying over one of the keyboards. Her dark hair was pulled up into a loose bun on her head and she wore a faded green T-shirt with a cat skateboarding. "I'll never say no to a good time, and sending the cops to the doorstep of some of these assholes is a very good time indeed." She shot a grin at Elliana.

Who returned her grin with an equally terrifying one.

"So… are you guys covering your tracks?" Because they were at his house and if they got caught, he wasn't sure how he'd explain the cops showing up here to Rebel.

Both women gave him dry looks before returning to their screens. Okay, so yes then. Not that he'd actually expected less, but he was strung tight.

"How's Rebel?" Lizzy asked.

"Good." More than, actually. She was handling things with so much calm and ease. "She's a boss," he added, because he was so damn impressed with her. And he wanted everyone to know how amazing she was.

His words earned him grins from both women but they didn't look up again.

"What did you want to show me?" If Elliana had asked him here, it meant that he was away from Rebel. To say he wasn't in a good mood because of that was an understatement. It didn't matter that she was safe, he was already itching to get back to her. To finish what they'd started.

"Hold on," Elliana murmured, working quickly on one of her laptops before she paused, then motioned for him to sit next to her. She turned the screen his way as he did and said, "There's a lot of info for us to sift through. So much it sort of hurts my brain. Thankfully there's a hashtag for her tour, and this concert weekend specifically, so we were able to grab a ton of footage from that alone. So far we've managed to link a few of the nastiest messages with a couple of potential stalkers. Including one asshole who had *front row* tickets to her concert last night. This guy." She pulled up a second screen, with a guy's face and specs listed.

Lizzy made a sound of disgust as she slightly leaned back in her chair and stretched. "He's got such a punchable face. Freaking weirdo."

Weston didn't say anything as he read over what Elliana had gathered. Ed Reeves. Twenty-six years old, had been arrested multiple times including on suspicion of taking pictures and videos up women's skirts in a public shopping area. Went to an Ivy League school on scholarships, parents deceased, no known relationship and was fired from his last job because of harassment complaints.

Weston hated him on sight. "You guys worked really fast. This is a lot of information."

"There's more," Lizzy murmured. "We're just starting to dive deep."

"Can you pull up the messages he sent?"

"Yeah." Elliana's fingers were a blur over her keyboard. "Only three of these are under his real name because he was stupid enough to leave messages from his main personal account. But after that he set up a handful of other accounts to troll her. Pathetic," she muttered as a new doc pulled up.

It listed the message and each social media platform where it had been posted.

"He cross-posts a lot of the same shit word for word." Weston managed to keep his tone even, but he saw red as he scanned the nastiness.

*You're a nasty whore who doesn't deserve anything. Everyone knows you're lip-syncing.*

*Did you gain weight? You looked like a cow at the concert in South Carolina.*

*I know you wore that blue dress for me in Tucson. Even if you look like a slut, I'll still take you.*

"Yeah, he wants to make sure she sees them apparently. Because she should care what some creepy rando says," Elliana growled, not bothering to keep the anger out of her voice.

"Jesus." Weston stopped reading halfway down, feeling sick. "Where is this guy now? Do you guys know?" Because their combined capability was scary.

"At home," Lizzy said. "And I've sent this video someone captured at the concert anonymously to the Miami PD. So he'll be getting a visit from them soon enough. Especially since I was kind enough to include his home address and name." She cackled but Weston couldn't join in.

Because forget the PD talking to this asshole. He now had the guy's name and address and had already made a decision. "Thank you, guys. I'll be back. Got my phone on me if you need me. If you get any more serious hits on local assholes, send me the info." He'd make the rounds today if needed.

"Uh, Weston?" Elliana's voice trailed after him as he strode from his office. "Damn it," she muttered, her voice fading as he made his way out the front door.

As he slid into the driver's seat of his Land Rover, Elliana raced at him, her blonde hair flying behind her before she jumped into the passenger seat. "Where the hell are you going?" she snapped as he started the engine.

"I think you know." He was going to personally visit the sick freak sending threatening messages to Rebel. He didn't care about the legality of anything at this point.

"Fine, but I'm going with you." When he started to argue, she held up a hand. "Not to stop you. But I want to make sure you don't do anything stupid. So if you leave me while I'm grabbing something from the back of my vehicle, I'll follow you and kick your ass later."

"I don't need—"

"Just shut up." She jumped from the seat but left the door open as she hurried to the back of her SUV.

He was surprised when she pulled a small drone out of the back, but moments later she slid back into the passenger seat, the mini drone and remote control in her lap.

"We can go now," she murmured.

"What's up with the drone?" He had an idea but wanted to confirm.

"Well, since you look super murdery, I think it's a good idea if I use a drone to check out his house, to see if there are any cameras or other security in the direct vicinity, including neighbors' homes. If you're going to mess this guy up, you're not getting caught by someone's doorbell camera or something."

Under normal circumstances, these were things he would have thought out clearly. "I'm not going to kill him." Probably.

Elliana snorted.

"I just keep seeing those messages. Who the hell does he think he is to talk to her like that?" He gripped the leather steering wheel, had to order his hands to loosen as he pulled out onto the quiet street. As he did, he saw Anthony heading toward Rebel's house, Bailey in the passenger seat. He half waved but didn't slow down.

Nothing was stopping him from confronting this asshole.

"You're surprisingly okay with me going to *not* murder this asshole," he finally said a few minutes later once they were on the main highway. Traffic was a beast, as always, and it would take longer than he'd like to get to the asshole's house, but there was nothing to do about it.

She lifted a shoulder, looked out the passenger window. "The people we love deserve to live in a world where they're not terrified of getting raped or killed by entitled assholes. I don't believe that following the letter of the law is always the right thing. The world isn't black and white. Something you already know."

Yeah, he did know. He'd served in Afghanistan with her and Van and the others who had formed their company. But he was closest with Elliana and Van for multiple reasons, one being that they'd bucked rules more than once, had followed their conscience instead of orders. And he had no regrets.

He'd kill for Rebel, die for her, do any damn thing to keep her safe from the monsters of the world.

"And I know how much Rebel cares for you and vice versa, even if I don't know her very well. I know *you*. I can't let you do something stupid and get caught," she added.

"You're a good friend," he murmured.

"So are you."

"Are you ever going to tell me why you like Rebel so much?"

Elliana groaned and turned the radio to low. "Fine, whatever. Nosy," she muttered. "When we were stuck in the sandbox, I... went through a bad breakup. Really bad. I never told you guys. Her music got me through it. Made me feel something other than pain, almost as if her words just tapped into my agony and let me know that everything would be okay eventually. That it didn't have to be okay now, but it would be in the future." She looked out the window again.

Weston slowed as he pulled off onto an exit. "That's it?"

"What do you mean, that's it? I just poured my soul out to you, ass face!"

"No, I mean, I thought maybe there was another reason."

"She kept me sane in that shithole. I mean, you and Van did too, obviously, but you know what I mean. I value that, and yeah, I'm kinda nuts about her music but whatever. I'm nuts about other things too."

"I just don't understand why you didn't tell me this earlier."

"Uh, because it's embarrassing."

"Embarrassing that you're human?"

"Definitely. I like people to think that I'm a badass robot with no emotions whatsoever."

He snort-laughed even with the heavy weight on his chest. "Well I think your secret is safe." Then he paused. "Who hurt you? Do I need to add them to my list of people to visit?"

She let out a bitter-sounding laugh. "Let's stick to one monster for now okay?"

"Fine, but I'm not letting this go." The low music on the radio filled the air as he made his way deeper into Miami.

"Does Rebel know what you're doing?" Elliana asked a few minutes later.

"Not specifically, no."

"Not specifically, or not at all?"

"I didn't tell her any of this. Nothing good comes with her knowing what I'm doing right now."

"That's a mistake. You should be honest with her."

"Are you giving me relationship advice now?"

"Yep," Elliana said, pulling her phone out when it buzzed. "So are you considering permanently taking over Rebel's security?"

"What's with all the questions?" Tension pulsed through him the closer they got to the address. The street they were on now had a lot of traffic, people pulling in and out of a packed shopping center.

"I'm feeling particularly nosy today. Especially since you've changed the last couple days."

"Changed?"

"Maybe not changed but you're finally making your move." There was approval in her voice as she responded to incoming texts.

"Fair enough, but I don't know. I'm taking over it for now. Her agent is doing a fine enough job, but..."

"No one will do a better job than you," she finished.

"Basically. After this tour ends, Rebel and I can figure things out. Oh," he added. "Did you look further into her assistant, Anna?"

"Yeah, she's fine. I mean, no weird financials, no weird anything. And this isn't her first time working with a celebrity. She comes highly recommended. Why'd you want me to run her anyway?"

That tension in his shoulders increased as he saw how close they were to the address of Ed Reeves. "She was acting jumpy around me."

Elliana snorted. "She's an assistant for a famous singer on the last leg of her tour and all of a sudden, said singer's scary boyfriend or whatever shows up and starts making changes, including the security. She's probably scared you're going to fire her or something."

He just shrugged. "We're a few blocks away. I'm going to drive by, then you and I will park and you can work your magic with the drone. Or I can." He had specialized training with them too.

She made a scoffing sound. "You're not touching Luna."

"You named your drone?" He slowed, made a turn into the neighborhood where Reeves lived.

"Of course. I name all my tech."

He knew she named her computers and her SUV but the drone seemed like overkill. "Why Luna?"

"Mainly because I use it at night to spy on my hot neighbor."

"What?" He shot her a quick glance as he made a right, deeper into the quiet neighborhood. There were a few two-story homes, but it was mainly one-story ranch-style homes, a lot of visible pools and immaculate lawns.

"He knows I do it. Usually puts on a show for me. Getting undressed, or in his shower. Sometimes he does a lot more though." And she sounded really pleased with that.

"Are you serious?"

"Yep. He's kind of a freak."

"Says the woman spying on her neighbor."

"I didn't say I wasn't a freak too."

"Are you guys like, dating then or what?"

"Nope."

"Have you ever talked to him like a normal human?"

"Kind of. I sat next to him at my neighborhood's last HOA meeting. I'm pretty sure they wouldn't approve of our nightly activities. Oh, and sometimes he'll wave at me when he's getting his mail. The way he smiles at me..." She made a fanning motion with her hand.

At that moment, Weston felt like his head might explode. "I don't even know how to respond to any of this." He turned onto Reeves's street, saw flashing lights.

Elliana shrugged, then froze. "Oh shit, looks like the PD beat us to it. Keep driving," she ordered, as if he'd planned to stop and have a chat with the police escorting Reeves to one of their cruisers. He also saw Detective Duarte.

"Shit," he muttered, pulling into a driveway and turning around. He didn't want to chance that the detective spotted him. He hadn't done anything illegal.

Yet.

But he didn't want to have to explain why he was in this neighborhood. Sure, he could say he was lost but that was pathetic and Duarte wouldn't buy it.

"They moved hella fast," Elliana murmured, glancing behind them.

Weston wasn't sure if that was a good or bad thing. Maybe a bit of both, because for how he was feeling, he wasn't certain he would have stuck to simply threatening the guy with words.

# CHAPTER 16

Weston stepped into Rebel's dressing room and nodded at Juan, who was standing at attention as one of Rebel's people finished applying some sort of sparkly stuff to her face. "Can Rebel and I have some privacy?"

Juan nodded and stepped outside to join Nash. The makeup artist ignored him as she finished up, then said, "You're perfect," with a smile to Rebel.

"Thanks Denise," she murmured. "You're an angel."

The older woman patted her shoulder gently, then gave Weston a curious look before she rolled her cart out of the dressing room.

"What's going on?" Weston asked, coming to stand near her vanity where she was currently eyeing herself.

And very intentionally ignoring him.

"What are you talking about?" Her tone was distracted, but he wasn't fooled. Nothing like the woman he'd kissed senseless just this morning, the one who'd been worried about his safety.

"I'm talking about the fact that you've been avoiding me since I got back to your place earlier." It had been hours, and yes, she'd been busy. And he wasn't being needy or whatever, that much he was sure of. He wasn't up in her space or begging for attention, but she'd been cold and distant. A complete one-eighty from where they'd been this morning, sending dirty texts.

She stood and shook out her silky robe, avoiding eye contact. "In case you haven't noticed, I'm getting busy for a big show and have a lot on my plate," she murmured before striding to the covered rolling cart of clothing.

"Damn it, Rebel. I know that. But I know something is going on and I can't fix it if you don't tell me what's wrong." And something was definitely wrong.

The door opened before Rebel could respond, if she was even going to, and Paige, Anna and one of the wardrobe people strode in. Manuel had been handling her wardrobe stuff for years. He smiled brightly at Weston, then even brighter at Rebel. "Have you looked yet?" he asked, his voice vibrating with excitement.

She laughed lightly, but he could see the tension around her eyes. "Not yet, I was just about to peek."

"Good, because I want to see your expression. I just finished some of these this morning," he said as he started unzipping the garment bag cover.

Anna had her phone out, was taking pictures, no doubt for social media. And Paige was talking into her headset.

Weston's window to talk to Rebel was closed and that was fine. For now. He'd figure out what was going on after the show. Because they were having this conversation and he was going to make things right.

Until then, he'd keep her safe.

As he started to step out of the room to join Nash and Juan, Rebel gasped.

He turned, saw her look of horror, and his gut curdled.

"Oh my god!" Manuel shouted. "What the hell is this!"

Weston frowned as ribbons of material floated to the ground, some of the dresses clearly having been slashed. "No one touch anything!" he snarled, striding forward. "And back up. Who brought this in here?" he demanded, looking around.

"I did," Anna whispered, her eyes brimming with tears. "But I just picked it up from the delivery guy."

"I had all this couriered over hours ago," Manuel said, staring in horror at the mess of fabric. "I... I..." He was shaking now, tears brimming in his eyes too.

Oh hell. There had to be a limited number of people who'd had access.

Weston looked at Paige, who had a similar look of shock. "Find a new room for Rebel. I'm going to call Detective Duarte in to see if his forensics can pick anything up from this." Though Weston was doubtful. Too many hands had been on it. "And I'm going to want to review the security feeds from the time you picked this up, to when it was brought here," he said, looking at Anna.

Rebel's assistant nodded, her tears gone now. "I didn't really check the outfits," she said, wincing as she glanced at Paige and Rebel. "The guy was in a rush to have me sign everything but I peeked at them. The clothes looked fine, but it wasn't like I inspected them."

Weston took a deep breath as he ordered himself to stay calm. He was livid this had happened and could only imagine how Rebel felt. She looked shocked but more than that, pissed. Her jaw was tight, but she was keeping her emotions in check.

"I'm going to need the name of the agency you used to courier everything over, and all their contact details," he said to Manuel, who nodded.

"Of course, of course. Anything you need. And Rebel, I've got some backups."

"I've got plenty of dresses to use from last night and some of our other shows." Her voice was even. "And I can just share a room with Lia, right?" she said, looking at Paige.

"Of course." Paige started barking orders into her headset as Juan and Nash stepped into the room.

"I know you both know this, but stick with her. No one gets too close to her now," Weston said quietly, a slow-burning rage buzzing through him. Someone wanted to hurt her, but they also wanted to scare her off her game. Everything about this felt personal.

He moved to Rebel, using his body to block her from everyone. Forcing her to look at him. "We're going to figure out who did this." And he was going to make them pay. "The police brought someone in earlier to talk to, but I don't know if he's still in custody."

She blinked. "They did?"

"Yeah, I'd planned to tell you after the concert." She hadn't seemed to want to talk at all prior, so he'd stayed in the background, focusing on her security.

"Oh." She took in a deep breath, seemed to center herself, then said, "I'm going to Lia's dressing room to start going over my new wardrobe, but if you find out anything else will you let me know?"

"Of course." He wanted to reach out, to comfort her, but she'd put a wall up between them. It didn't matter that it was invisible, it was still impenetrable. He hated it. If there weren't half a dozen other people in the room, and if he didn't have security shit to deal with, he'd demand answers. Instead, he simply cupped her cheek gently. "I'm going to figure out who did this."

She leaned into his touch for a moment, then nodded, giving him a tight smile before she headed off with Juan and Nash. He had his cell out as soon as she was gone, and called Duarte's private cell. He wanted to keep this as quiet as possible for now.

This had been meant to hurt her, maybe even hurt her performance. It was too personal, too nasty.

And he was damn sure going to find the perpetrator.

***

"She's good. About to go on," Juan said into the earpiece. "Some of our people did another security check of the stage and rafters too."

Weston could hear the crowd in the background as if through a tunnel as he listened to Juan. He was still in the security room scanning the footage from when the dresses had been delivered. "I'll be out there in a few."

Detective Duarte looked over his shoulder at him. "What?"

"Talking to Juan." Weston tapped his earpiece and the detective looked back at the screen as he finished downloading all the security footage.

He was taking it with him so his people could go over everything but the two of them had watched Anna sign off on the delivery of costumes, then walk it to Rebel's dressing room. But before that, she'd made a few stops and some were out of the scope of the cameras, unfortunately. Weston had also downloaded a copy of everything for himself before the detective got there and had sent it to Elliana and Lizzy.

"I doubt we're going to get any viable prints," the detective murmured as he stood. "Maybe on the rolling cart itself but I have a feeling we'll be pulling prints from people at the designer's place and people who work here. If whoever did this was smart enough to do it before the delivery, they wore gloves."

"What's the deal on the delivery person?"

"I haven't located him yet—it's only been an hour," he added. "Detective work takes time and we're working a lot of angles." He cleared his throat and looked around the security room, lowered his voice so the two men on the other side of the room wouldn't overhear. "We brought someone in for questioning today."

Weston only nodded, not letting on that he'd known that. "And?"

"And, he's sent some nasty messages to Rebel. Not enough to charge him with anything."

"So he's still in custody?"

"Unfortunately no, but I'm going to suggest to Ms. Martinez that she file a restraining order. She can keep him from getting too close to her."

Not even close to good enough. "Restraining orders are bullshit."

The detective lifted a shoulder, but didn't deny it. "It's something on file and if he breaks the order, we can arrest him."

Yeah, but then hold him for how long? Weston bit his tongue and simply nodded. He certainly wasn't going to tell the detective that he planned to handle this guy himself if he posed a real threat to Rebel. That asshole wasn't going to get the chance to hurt her. Nope. "Could he have destroyed her costumes today?" Weston asked. If he had, it meant he'd been at the concert venue and that shouldn't have happened. Not with the security they had in place. But even Weston could admit that this place was an absolute madhouse with far too many entrances.

"It's possible. I put someone on him and they said he went home and stayed home. But... I don't know. Anything is possible."

Weston nodded again. "Okay, well, thank you."

Duarte eyed him as he tucked his paperwork away. "I'm going to tell you this once because I recognize that look in your eyes and I know from Grant that you've got military experience."

After some digging, he'd found out that Grant Caldwell, had once been partners with Duarte and trusted the guy with his life. That went a long way in vouching for the guy's capability. "Okaaay." He stretched out the word, wondering where the hell this was going.

"Don't do anything stupid. Don't go after someone you *think* might be involved in this. Let me and the Miami PD do our job. If you interfere, you could get hurt or hurt someone innocent. And the last thing I want to do is have to arrest you. Understood?"

He gave his most neutral smile. "Of course, detective. I'm not leaving Rebel's side or vicinity in the near future. And I would never think of interfering with an investigation."

The detective's mouth pulled into a thin line, the man clearly not believing Weston. But he simply nodded once and said, "Contact me if you need me. If not, I'll be in touch." Then he stalked off.

Weston followed after him but veered in another direction toward the main stage. The stadium was packed and he could hear the crowd singing along to a familiar tune. One of Rebel's first hits. It was upbeat, about a woman coming into her own, easy to dance to, and had likely been played by hundreds of thousands of people at clubs and parties. Maybe more. Hell, definitely more.

As he passed the line of dressing rooms, he saw Anna coming out of Lia and now Rebel's temporary dressing room, a vase of roses in her hands.

"Is everything okay?" she asked him as she strode down the hall, her heels clicking away. "With the detective I mean?"

"Yep. He's got a few leads."

"Good, good. I'm still pissed about what happened. At myself and whoever did this. I should have checked her clothes," she ground out, stopping at a room that had a conference table with a dozen chairs surrounding it and some of the stage people eating sandwiches. She set the roses on the table. "Whoever wants these can have them," she said, before striding out.

He followed after her, wanting to dig a little deeper. "Do you have any idea who could have done that to her clothes?"

Anna sighed and lifted a shoulder as they reached the end of the hallway. The music was louder now as they got closer to the stage area. "Honestly, I could think of half a dozen people who don't like her, but it's based on jealousy, not anything of substance. And what happened is... well, it seems extreme, even for show business. And risky." She lifted her shoulder again. "I can't speculate on this, I've got too many things to do, especially since her last show of the tour is tomorrow. If you need me, I've got my cell on me," she said, moving away from him before he could respond.

After checking in with Juan and Nash, he headed back the way Anna had come and knocked on Lia's dressing room door. There was a Red Stone Security employee he vaguely recognized posted outside. Just like they were supposed to be, good.

"Come in!" Lia called out.

"Hey." He hovered in the doorway since he didn't know her well and didn't want to invade her space, even if she was sharing it with Rebel.

She looked surprised to see him. "Everything okay? Does the detective need to talk to me again?"

"Ah, no. I'm just doing a sweep of the place." He hoped his tone was casual enough. "Is Anna your assistant too?"

Lia snorted dismissively as she continued packing up her small duffle bag. "No. She can barely keep up with Rebel. No way could she handle two of us."

"Okay, thanks." He'd wanted to get the other singer's take on Anna, but looked like that wasn't happening.

"And I'm pretty sure she's job hunting." Lia zipped her bag and hefted it up. "At least that's the buzz I've been hearing. Probably for the best since she clearly can't keep up with this fast-paced business." She rolled her eyes. "If you don't need me, I'm getting out of here. It's been a long day and I'm ready to crash."

"Of course." He stepped back out and murmured to the woman standing security. "Check the ID of anyone who comes in here. If it's not Paige, Anna or Rebel, no one needs to be in here. If they insist, alert me."

The dark-haired woman nodded. "Of course."

Knowing that Rebel's temporary dressing room was as safe as it could be, he finally headed toward the stage. He loved seeing her perform, loved hearing her.

And tonight, once they were finally alone, he was going to find out why she'd tried to put up walls between them today. Because that shit wasn't happening.

They'd crossed a line and he wasn't going back, wasn't going to be put into a little box again.

# CHAPTER 17

Rebel was beyond exhausted as she wrapped her wet hair up into a turban. The show had gone well even without the original wardrobe. Because it wasn't about her clothing, but the content.

Still.

She was angry that someone had done that to her, felt almost violated. It was just... mean. She knew that the world was full of shitty people and today had been a reminder. But the world was also full of incredibly generous, giving people, like all her fans who'd actually paid to come see her perform. There was no way she would let them down by letting the recent incidents affect her performance.

It was just so hard to get out of her head sometimes, to remember the good outweighed the bad. "And you're just avoiding thinking about Weston," she muttered to herself. After she went through her evening routine, then braided her damp hair, she slid a robe on and stepped into her bedroom.

And found Weston there.

She stopped inside the threshold. "Oh..."

"You think I'm just going home after today?" His jaw was set tight and oh, he was definitely angry at her.

Probably because she'd been avoiding him all afternoon. "Weston—"

"No. If you want me to leave, fine, I'll sleep in one of the guest rooms. But what the hell is going on? Things were great between us, then I come back and..." He made an explosion motion with his hands. "You won't even talk to me."

Guilt gnawed at her. She knew she should have just talked to him, but she was the queen of avoidance. And oh boy, she'd been feeling insecure after what her bestie had told her. "Anthony saw you leaving your house with a hot blonde. Sounded a lot like Elliana. And you wouldn't tell me where you were going," she blurted. "I thought you were maybe doing something dangerous but then it turns out that you were..." Well, she didn't know what he'd been doing, but jealousy ate her alive and she absolutely hated that. She didn't want to be that person, but thinking about him with someone else, or lying to her... Ugh.

He blinked, then laughed, though without humor. "That's why you've been icing me out?"

"You were leaving your house with her! Has she been like, staying there?"

He scrubbed a hand over his face and she saw how tired he looked for the first time. Guilt pricked at her. "No, she wasn't staying there. I mean, I asked her over this morning but..." He paced a little, seemed to struggle with himself, then stopped and faced her.

"I asked her over because I needed help hacking some stuff. Her and..." He cleared his throat. "Someone else who's name I can't say. They're good at finding things out. Then when they got some information on that asshole Ed Reeves who's been sending you nasty messages, I decided to go pay him a visit. He was at your concert in the front row Friday night." Weston took an angry step forward, though it was clear his anger wasn't focused on her, but the jackass who was brave behind his keyboard. "That piece of shit was at your concert so close he could have jumped up there and touched you. And the messages he's been sending you are vile."

She stared at him for a long moment. "*Wait*, you were going to do what to him?"

"I don't honestly know. Probably more than talk to him. But the police beat me to the punch and were bringing him in for questioning before I could get to him. And the only reason Elliana was with me is because she jumped into my vehicle at the last minute because she was worried I'd do something stupid. She wanted to make sure I didn't get arrested."

"Oh..." Rebel was moving before she'd even processed it, had her arms around him tight, her face buried against his chest. God, she was so embarrassed. And okay, relieved. "I'm sorry for assuming the worst. I just... I've never been jealous before! But I got up in my head and I'm just sorry. I trust you, and I promise not to act like an asshole again. Or at least I'll work on it. I'm so embarrassed," she whispered. And angry at herself because she knew Weston, knew he wouldn't lie to her. But she'd let stupid insecurities eat her alive.

His grip around her was tight. "You're not mad about what I was doing?"

"I'm still sort of processing that." She leaned back slightly to look up at him. "You can't go after people who send me ugly messages, you know that, right?"

"I do know that. But there's a bit more to it with him. He's stalking you."

She sighed but didn't let him go. "I feel like such an asshole for avoiding you today." She'd been trying to protect herself. To step back mentally and emotionally so his betrayal would hurt less. She should have trusted him.

"In the future, can we talk instead of making assumptions?" he murmured, cupping her cheek gently.

"Definitely. You're probably going to have to remind me. I'm really, really good at avoiding confrontation." She winced as she said it. "I know it's terrible and I'm working on it but clearly I have a ways to go." It was a protective mechanism she'd learned as a little girl.

"Just don't run from me or hide from me." His expression was so sincere as he stroked his thumb over her cheek. "I can't stand it."

"Okay. I promise," she whispered, tightening her grip around him as her heart rate kicked up. He smelled so damn good and the heated look in his blue eyes pierced her right to her core. She wanted to forget all about today and lose herself with him.

His gaze fell to her mouth and heat arced between them. She wasn't sure who moved first, but suddenly they were kissing, hot and hard, and she clutched onto him as he pinned her to the bed.

They definitely weren't going to stop at kissing this time. Or she hoped they weren't.

His big hand slid between their bodies, and she could feel him untying her robe as he nipped her bottom lip. "This okay?"

"Everything you do is okay." She wanted it clear that she didn't want to stop. She'd been fantasizing about him for years and relief that he hadn't been lying to her was riding her hard. She didn't want to be afraid anymore. Not when it came to Weston. She wanted to be brave and go for what she wanted—she certainly did in her professional life. Now she needed to transfer it to her personal one.

He groaned against her mouth as he cupped one of her bare breasts. She whimpered as he slowly rolled her already hard nipple between his thumb and forefinger, gently teasing her.

Heat rushed between her legs as he lazily played with one nipple, then the other, seemingly content to take his time. Meanwhile, she felt as if she was going to combust. This was like years in the making, at least for her, and yeah, she could tell it was for him too.

She reached between their bodies and made quick work of his button and zipper. "Pants off now," she growled against his mouth.

She wanted to see what she'd been fantasizing about for years. Though she knew it had to be better than her dreams.

He laughed against her, his big body shaking with it, and the sound warmed her from the inside out. "Yes ma'am," he murmured, mock saluting as he leaned back and shucked his pants and boxer briefs with little dogs on them. How was he hot and adorable at the same time? This man should come with a warning label.

Ooooh, my. She stared up at him as he stood at the edge of the bed, looking down at her. "Shirt too. All of it," she whispered. Because she wanted all of him.

His blue eyes went molten as he stared at her, his gaze roving from her head to purple-painted toenails. "If I'm getting naked, you are too."

Her robe was half off with one breast out already, but she sat up slightly. All she had to do was slide her arms out of the silky material, letting it pool beneath her on the bed.

He sucked in a sharp breath, his eyes heating up even more. "I've fantasized about you more times than I should admit," he said as he started peeling his shirt over his head. It was like he was moving in slow motion for her benefit, revealing muscled inch after muscled inch.

Another wave of heat punched through her as she stared her fill, looked at the sharp planes of his abs, the way his biceps flexed as he tossed his shirt to the ground. Her brain was going into overload as she drank in every inch of him. How was his body even real? And when her gaze landed on his thick erection... Holy wow. "You're beautiful," she murmured, her eyes firmly on his cock.

He laughed lightly, his cock bobbing slightly as he crawled onto the bed. "I'm glad you think so but I've got nothing on you."

Grinning, she scooted back farther on the bed, was glad when he followed, caging her in beneath him. "For the record, I've fantasized about you over the years too." Like a lot. But she held that little bit back. She arched her breasts up to meet his chest, the skin to skin making her shudder in anticipation.

"Rebel," he murmured, cupping her cheek, but then he kissed her instead of continuing.

And she was glad because right now she didn't need words. She just needed all of him.

Spreading her legs wide, she wrapped them around him, stroking her heels over his ass and the backs of his legs with a compulsion to touch him everywhere. Hands, feet, whatever, didn't matter. She wanted to imprint herself on him, make sure that every inch of him was touched by her. She was possessive like that.

He was her addiction and now that she was getting a real taste... She stroked her hands up over his chest, back down—

"Wrap your hand around my cock," he growled into her mouth, even as he cupped her mound, slid a finger along her slick folds.

Ooooh, she really liked that commanding tone. She'd planned to tease him a little, but had no problem giving him exactly what he wanted. And there wasn't much she wouldn't give this man. Even if he broke her heart, she was giving it to him anyway. Wasn't like she had much of a choice at this point. He already owned it, even if he didn't realize it.

She wrapped her fingers around his thick length, stroked once, then ran her thumb along the smooth head of his cock oh so softly.

He groaned as he slid two fingers inside her, stretching her. "Honey, I changed my mind. No touching or I'm going to come."

Grinning, she stroked him again and he nipped her bottom lip harder.

"Rebel," he growled, grasping both her hands, drawing them above her head as he pinned her in place.

His thick length pressed against her opening as she spread her thighs wider, rolled her hips to meet his. Oh... "Condom!" she blurted.

He blinked, cursed again. "In my SUV. I'm the biggest dumbass in the world." The words seemed to be torn from him as he stared down at her.

And she felt that impatience all the way to her core, because no way was she letting him stop this long enough for him to go to his car. Those condoms might as well be on Mars. "I'm on the Pill. If you've been tested recently—"

"I have. I'm clean. It's been a while, Rebel." He looked as if he wanted to say more, but held back.

It had been soooo very long for her. With her schedule, dating was damn near impossible and she didn't do one-night stands. But that all seemed unnecessary to say. "For me too. Like years. And I'm clean too but only if you're sure—"

He crushed his mouth to hers, answering her question, and slid inside her, his thick erection filling her completely as he thrust deep.

She arched up, the sensation of him filling her almost too much, for reasons she didn't want to think about. He was the only man she'd ever loved, even if she'd never told him. The man she compared every other one to.

Because he'd always been there for her, always been a rock. To be with him like this now was more than she'd ever hoped for. In the back of her mind, she'd always been scared to imagine a future with him. Because that led to her wanting that reality with a desperation that scared her.

She began rolling her hips against his as they picked up their pace, almost feeling frantic. Every time he thrust into her, he hit that elusive spot deep inside and she moved closer and closer to climax. So apparently even his dick was perfect and he was going to ruin her for anyone else. Not that there would be anyone else. Nope, he was it for her, even if she didn't want to fully acknowledge it.

Her nipples beaded tight, her entire body balancing on a tightrope of pleasure as the man she'd been dreaming about for years thrust inside her again. And again and again, over and over, filling her completely.

And when he reached between their bodies and began teasing her clit, the pleasure that had been building slammed out to all her nerve endings in a rush of sensations.

She grabbed onto his butt, holding him tight as he continued thrusting inside her. She knew he was close; all the muscles in his body were pulled tight, his breathing harsh.

"Let go," she ordered quietly, staring up into his gorgeous, strained face. She wanted him to let go, to mark her, claim her, even if she couldn't put those thoughts into words. It was what she wanted with every fiber of her being.

He crushed his mouth to hers again and did as she said, coming inside her, his body trembling as he found his own release.

She stroked her fingers down his spine as she looked up at his face. His expression was softer than she'd ever seen it.

"Next time will be a lot longer," he murmured.

She smiled. "I'm glad there's going to be a next time."

"Too many to count, Rebel. You're mine." He brushed his lips over hers, then eased back, groaning slightly as he pulled out of her. "Sit tight."

Like she was going anywhere? As he hurried to her bathroom she stayed where she was, staring up at the high ceiling of her bedroom, and replayed those words in her head.

*Too many to count.* She certainly hoped so. She wanted to learn everything that made him tick, to kiss all over his body, to give him pleasure everywhere in this house. And his. She wanted to claim him for the entire world to see, even as she worried he wasn't ready for it.

For all the baggage that brought along. And it was heavy.

Even with the knowledge of all that baggage, she still wanted a future with him. To wake up to his face every day, a wedding, a family, all the bells and whistles. Because she couldn't settle for less.

Before she could fall even deeper down the rabbit hole of her thoughts, he was back with a wet washcloth, kneeling next to her on the bed.

She watched him as he gently cleaned between her legs, wondered how such a big man could be so gentle and had to shove back another wave of emotions. Because crying after sex? Yeah, not happening.

"Any regrets?" he asked her once he'd tossed the washcloth back into her bathroom and slid into bed with her.

"None." She curled up against him, laying her head on his chest as he wrapped his arms around her.

She wanted this to last. Needed it to. With him, she felt safe and protected in a way she'd never felt anywhere else, or with anyone else. He was like her home. The shift from friends to lovers should have felt weird, but it didn't. Not even a little. Everything about tonight felt so damn perfect.

And that terrified the hell out of her. Because things would never be the same for them now. There was no going back.

Not that she wanted to. But that little voice in her head, the one full of self-loathing and constant doubt, was egging her on, telling her this was too good to last. That she'd eventually lose him and then she'd have no one.

She pushed the voice down, silencing her as she moved even closer to Weston. She was holding onto him for as long as he was willing to stay. And she would fight for a future with him.

# CHAPTER 18

She looked at her phone. Eight in the morning. And she'd barely slept, had been too wired, which meant she'd likely get no sleep at all now. Frustrated, she pulled out a small bottle of amphetamines a friend had sold to her. Looked like she'd be taking these all day. Again. But there was no way around it. Not when there was so much to be done before tonight.

She was going to stop Rebel once and for all.

She hadn't been fazed at all last night. After what had happened with the show the night before, she'd thought Rebel would cancel for sure.

But no, the show had gone off without a hitch. Even without her new wardrobe, the bitch had performed perfectly. Now even more opportunities were rolling in for her.

She deserved none of it.

Clearly something had to give—she needed to take more drastic measures. Tomorrow was Rebel's last show of the tour. That might be the last time she was close enough to stop her.

To take away from her all the things she didn't deserve. Ungrateful, untalented bitch.

Decision made, she pulled out a burner phone she'd bought a week ago and called someone.

"Yeah?" Ed Reeves answered, the sound of clicking on a keyboard in the background.

"Mr. Reeves? This is Rebel Martinez's assistant, Anna Cook."

The line went silent and she had to check her screen to see if the loser had hung up. "Are you there?" she asked sweetly.

"Why are you calling me?"

"We'd like to invite you to do a backstage tour tonight after the big show. That is if you're available."

More silence. "I thought she wanted to file a restraining order against me." His words were hesitant, but there was just a hint of hope. *What a freakshow.*

"That's all just a misunderstanding. She's read your messages and wants to hear what you have to say. She values the opinions of all her fans and she knows that you've bought tickets to so many of her shows. It won't just be you, there will be a handful of others invited. But it sounds like you're not interested, so—"

"No! I mean yes, I'm interested. I'm just surprised is all."

He was so gross and creepy. Rebel deserved him and all her other deranged fans. "You and a few others will be picked up by a driver and let in the back. It's all very VIP, so you can't tell anyone about it."

"Of course." He sounded more enthusiastic now. "Whatever you need."

"Do you have a pen?" she asked, smiling to herself. This would put Rebel over the edge and make her afraid to ever take the stage again. "I don't want you to forget anything."

"Uh, yeah! Hold on."

Leaning back in her chair, she smiled wider. Tonight was going to be one no one would ever forget.

Rebel was finally going to get what was coming to her.

# CHAPTER 19

Holding Rebel against the shower wall, his cock deep inside her, Weston slowly teased her clit, feeling her inner walls tighten around him with each flick of his thumb.

"I can't believe I'm going to come again," she rasped out, her head falling on his shoulder, her entire body shuddering as he increased the pressure of his thumb.

"You can do it," he whispered. "Just let go." He'd woken her up this morning with his head between her legs, and then joined her in the shower.

Because he was addicted and just like the lyrics to one of her songs, he couldn't get enough.

She held onto him tight as the water pounded down around them, the only sound other than their harsh breathing in the tile and glass enclosure.

He gently squeezed her clit and she suddenly jerked against him, her climax starting to crest.

He massaged her clit harder as he ground his hips into hers, keeping his cock buried inside her, filling her, hitting that sweet spot that made her moan.

"Weston!" She clutched onto him as she started coming again, water pouring down the both of them as he continued pleasuring her.

Making her come at least once a day was his main life goal now and until the end of time. Seeing the blissed-out expression on her face as her head fell back when she came from his touch was everything.

Holding on to his shoulders, she looked at him, her eyes heavy lidded. Then she rolled her hips, a silent demand. "I'm not the only one getting dessert this morning."

Grinning, he pulled back and thrust into her hard, savored the way she groaned out his name as if he was the only man who existed.

He lost all sense of time as he thrust into her over and over, all his muscles pulled taut as he held her up against the wall, losing himself inside her. When she dug her nails into his back, he climaxed hard, his entire body trembling as he came inside her. Filling her. Marking her as his.

"I wish we could stay here all day," she murmured as she let her legs drop from around him, gently smoothing her hands over his chest.

He loved it when she touched him, but he swore he could feel her pulling away from him emotionally, even though they were still entwined together in her shower. He refused to get up in his head though. "Me too."

Sighing, she laid her head against his chest, her face turned away from pouring water.

Weston wrapped his arms around her, smoothed his hands up and down her back. This stolen time was precious. He didn't want it to end. "What's going on in that gorgeous head of yours?"

"Just thinking about the real world, that's all." There was a note of sadness in her voice.

He tightened his grip. "If you're worried about me, don't. I'm not going anywhere."

"I'm not worried about you," she said, finally raising her head to look up at him. "Just worried how tough it will be for you to adjust to life in the spotlight. You know, I mean, if we... ah, you and I make things official."

He blinked, taken off guard by her doubt. "We *are* official. I'm not dating anyone else and neither are you," he snapped out a hell of a lot harsher than he'd intended.

She blinked, then gave him a soft smile, followed by a laugh. "Okay then. I'm just saying it's going to be a lot. It's actually why I didn't put that picture I took of us on social media. The one with me kissing your cheek. I was worried that people would start harassing you and questioning our relationship. And that was even before…" She motioned between the two of them.

"Post it. Post anything. I want the entire goddamn world to know you're mine. I'm not going anywhere, Rebel."

She stared up at him, her dark amber eyes wide. He wasn't sure how she could doubt him, doubt them.

He crushed her to him now, claiming her mouth hard, trying to banish the shadows he saw in her eyes. But he wasn't sure it was enough to completely erase her worry and fear. The only thing that would do that was time, not pretty words from him.

Good thing he had a lot of it and wasn't going anywhere. He'd show her that he was in this for the long run, that the invasion of his privacy wasn't going to scare him off. If anything, this was the ultimate challenge because he'd built his new career on giving others privacy.

He'd keep her, keep them, safe from the world.

*** 

Still in her workout gear, Rebel strode into the kitchen and wasn't surprised to find Juan waiting with Weston at the countertop. "I see they found something to eat," she murmured to Nash, who'd gone running with her.

Her bodyguard simply grinned. He was definitely the quieter of the two, but she was wearing him down. She'd learned that he was happily married and that talking about his wife was a good subject to make him open up a bit. The woman had a fascinating job handling antiquities and Rebel hoped that she got to meet her.

Both Weston and Juan turned toward them, but only Weston's gaze swept over her as if he wanted to eat her right up. "How was the run?"

"Great," she said, feeling invigorated. Though that probably had something to do with the sex from earlier as well. Damn it, and now she could feel her cheeks flushing. Gah. And now she'd need another shower before leaving because she'd decided to get a solid run around the track on the back of her property so she could focus. Five miles later and she was ready for the final show.

Ready to put on the best show yet, and then after... Take things slow for a bit. Or slow for her. Adopt Jupiter and Lucky. Give them the home and love they deserved. And see where things went with Weston. She knew exactly where she wanted them to go but was worried if she told him everything she wanted, it would freak him out. She needed to just take things one day at a time.

*Not* ask him to move in with her.

Because that would be bonkers.

"Did you manage to keep up?" Juan asked Nash before taking a sip of his coffee. His empty plate sat behind him.

"He did great, and you don't get to give him grief when you won rock paper scissors. Next time you're running with me."

Juan groaned slightly but was grinning as he did. "Fine, but I hope *you* can keep up."

Nash simply shook his head, but Weston was watching her closely. His eyes might be ice blue, but the look in them was scorching.

She snorted and headed for the fridge, but Weston was faster, grabbed her a water bottle. "Thanks," she murmured.

He simply nodded. "Paige is on her way over, ready to go over some things before we all head out."

That familiar tension built at the back of her head and along her shoulders, almost making her run pointless. She rolled her shoulders once and wondered if she had time for another shower before her agent got there. Or if she'd have to wait. "What were you guys up to while I was gone, other than eating?" she asked pointedly.

Weston just grinned. "Mainly eating. Your chef left some incredible premade stuff."

"I know. If it wasn't for him, I'd be eating ramen or takeout." As it was, having a chef prep all her food made staying healthy a lot easier. And during a tour, she worked at staying in top form. The shows took all of her energy, so she had to be in good shape physically and mentally. Which was why she needed to stop worrying about her stalker. Easier said than done, of course.

"Your agent is here." Nash's voice was low as he set the tablet with all the shots of the security cameras on the island top.

Rebel had a feeling that she knew why Paige was here so early. They didn't need to get together at all until this afternoon. But she'd been putting her agent off about future stuff for weeks and now it was time to pay the piper, apparently.

"Thanks. Can you guys let her in and then just hang out until I'm ready to go? I need some privacy for a bit."

They both nodded and disappeared out of the kitchen.

"I'm not going anywhere," Weston murmured, planting himself at the island.

"I didn't ask you to."

"Just making sure we're on the same page."

"Are you looking for an argument or something?"

He snorted softly. "No. Just don't want you thinking you can get rid of me.'"

"Weston…" She paused at the sound of Paige's heels coming from the hallway. As she waited, she drank half of her water and reminded herself that saying no was always an option. It was just hard for her sometimes. Okay, all the time.

Because she got FOMO and worried that she'd miss out on a great opportunity. Which meant she often said yes to things and then regretted it later because she was so burned out. She'd been getting a lot better though over the last year and just had to stick to her plan.

"Hey, you two." Paige strode in wearing a formfitting navy-blue dress with strappy heels and her sunglasses pushed back on her head. Her long, wavy caramel-colored hair was perfect as always. "Are you ready for tonight?"

"Yep. Just got in a run and might do some light weight reps before my shower. I'm feeling it for tonight. Do we have any news on the wardrobe?"

"Manuel has replicated about half of the outfits that were destroyed and will be delivering them to you personally this afternoon. I think you should just stay in Lia's dressing room tonight too. I know I'm being superstitious, but after yesterday it feels like bad luck to go back into yours."

"Agreed." She felt weird going back into her dressing room after yesterday and didn't want to tempt fate.

Weston frowned as he looked between the two of them. "There's no such thing as luck."

She and Paige both shook their heads practically in unison.

"Don't say that," she whispered. "Something you should understand is that entertainers are all superstitious. So don't throw that out into the universe."

He looked mildly amused, but just shrugged as she turned back to her agent.

"So... I know why you're here, and the answer is still no."

Paige's megawatt smile didn't dim a watt. "I know, I know. It's too soon to plan another tour and I know you said no to a Vegas residency. But I was thinking that you might want to at least do a month of shows there, get a feel for what it might be like if you ever decide to. You loved it when you were there a few months ago."

Vegas had been one of her stops and she had enjoyed some aspects of it, especially her stay at the Serafina hotel. "Miami is my home. I'm not moving there, and I just want to get through tonight before I think about anything else."

"I know, but—"

"Paige," Weston interrupted her as he slid off his stool. "Rebel needs a shower and to go over some stuff. But I wanted to talk to you about some security things on your way out." He looked at Rebel, nodded once. "I'll join you later," he murmured as he expertly guided Paige out.

Rebel could see that her agent wanted to argue, but she took the opportunity to basically run from the kitchen. Weston was really good at handling people, at taking charge. She needed to get better at it but damn, having him just take over like that when he saw she was frustrated was insanely hot.

Maybe she shouldn't like it so much, but she made so many damn decisions every day that she appreciated how well he'd just fit into her life. He knew her better than anyone and she trusted him with her privacy. Not to mention he had his own money. She wasn't worried about him wanting to be with her for the wrong reasons.

She hoped that she fit well into his life too. After this concert, she wanted to meet more of his friends. To do normal couple things together.

To spend all her free time with him—and her new pups, who she couldn't wait to officially adopt. But first she had to get through tonight.

After that, she had no real commitments lined up and couldn't wait to take a break for the first time in over a decade.

# CHAPTER 20

Rebel turned as Weston stepped into the opening of her shower. He stayed back since he was still dressed, figuring she was almost done anyway.

The smile on her face punched right through to his core, even more than seeing her completely naked. "Fancy seeing you here again," she said as she turned the knob off. The pure joy on her expression as she watched him nearly brought him to his knees. He loved this woman. Always had.

Even though she was smiling, he found he couldn't smile back as he handed her the little towel he knew she used for drying her hair. And he also couldn't stop staring as drops of water glistened over her entire body, making her practically glow.

Jesus, there had never been anyone as beautiful as her. Her bathroom was massive with a ton of natural light coming in from the rectangular windows along the top of the walls. And right now she looked like a glowing goddess as she stepped toward him.

"What's with the frown?" she murmured, starting to take the towel.

But he started drying her instead, savoring being able to take care of her. To touch her while it was just the two of them and no one else. "Just annoyed with Paige. I know she's a great agent, she's just annoyingly pushy," he grumbled.

She snickered slightly. "Uh, yeah, it's why she's so damn good at her job. She doesn't like the word no. But it doesn't matter. I'm not doing Vegas or planning another tour yet. I'm looking forward to adopting my two pups and being able to actually relax at home. I bought this place and feel like I'm never here. I've been killing myself for twelve years straight and while I have no regrets, I need a break."

He wanted to ask where he fit into her plans, but for the life of him couldn't find the words. He had no problem taking over things, but when it came to Rebel it was different. As he started drying between her legs, he gently rubbed the towel over her clit.

She hitched in a breath, reached out to steady herself by clutching onto his shoulders as he dropped the towel. "I don't think we have time," she whispered, but didn't step back.

Oh, they had time for this. He would always have time for her pleasure, and he wanted her to know that she always came first. He stepped forward, forcing her backward until her back pressed up against the tile.

Then he went down on his knees.

Her eyes widened, but so did her legs. She spread her thighs as she stared down at him and he wondered if she was even aware of opening her legs for him. "Good girl," he murmured.

And oh, she liked that. Her dark amber eyes dilated as he slid a hand up her calf, gently massaging her toned leg as he lifted it, guided it over his shoulder.

She gasped slightly, as if she was surprised, but she had to know what he planned. He was tasting her, making her come, and leaving no doubt that she was his.

And they had plenty of time. She was the boss. Everyone could wait for her as far as he was concerned.

He nipped at her inner thigh, smiled against her soft skin when she jolted slightly. "I love how reactive you are," he murmured against her skin, gently scraping his teeth along the sensitive area. To be fair, he loved everything about her.

She rolled her hips again even as she slid her fingers through his hair. "Quit teasing me." A breathy demand.

"I'll take all the time I want." He kept his voice pitched low as he slowly ran his finger along the seam of her slick folds.

She was so damn wet that he shuddered with hunger, his cock straining against his pants already. Though he'd been hard since the moment he'd stepped into her open shower and seen her standing there naked.

Spreading her folds, he looked up at her. "Is this all for me?"

She nodded, her expression a little dazed and a lot hungry. For him.

Still watching her, he slid a finger inside her, inwardly smiled in triumph as she trembled, her head rolling back against the tile. "I can't help it, you make me crazy," she murmured.

"Welcome to my entire life," he growled against her wetness, flicking his tongue against her clit. Because she'd been making him crazy since they were teenagers.

Then he stopped talking and began teasing. He was getting her off before she had to go to work. Maybe more than once.

Her fingers tightened against his head, the bite of pain perfect as he brought her pleasure.

"Weston," she groaned out.

And hell, his cock kicked against his pants as she said his name in that worshipful tone.

"You have a magic mouth," she continued. "Oh god!" She stretched the word out as he sucked on the sensitive bundle of nerves, her entire body trembling.

"Not god. Just Weston," he growled against her slick folds.

"Oh my god," she laugh-cried as he sucked again. "Don't make me laugh." Then she seemed to forget how to talk as he continued thrusting his fingers inside her while massaging her clit.

It didn't take long until she came apart under his mouth, until her orgasm slammed into her as she murmured sweet things to him.

At that moment, he felt as if he'd died and gone to Heaven. If there was one, it was with Rebel. Because he didn't want any life where she wasn't in it. Standing, he cupped her mound as he claimed her mouth with his.

She wrapped her entire body around his as she met his tongue stroke for stroke, leaned into him and claimed him right back. Or maybe that was wishful thinking on his part. He'd wanted her for as long as he could remember, and he'd sort of bulldozed his way into her life now. Because he'd do anything to keep her safe. He just hoped this was a long-term thing for her because he couldn't go back to the way things had been before.

"Now it's your turn," she whispered as she pulled back, her dark eyes mischievous as she rubbed her palm over his covered cock.

He sucked in a breath at her soft touch. "No, this was just about you."

"You're not the only one who's bossy," she said as she pulled the button free on his pants.

He wanted to tell her to stop, that he'd just wanted this to be about her. But then she reached into his pants and wrapped her fingers around his cock tightly.

Aaaaand, he wasn't stopping anything. She stroked him softly at first, but her grip grew progressively harder, faster, and each time he groaned, she seemed to know exactly what pressure he wanted.

Then she took him completely by surprise and shoved his pants fully down and dropped to her knees.

"Rebel…"

She looked up at him, an eyebrow raised in challenge. She might be on her knees, but she was definitely in control. "You don't want this?"

He couldn't find the words to say no because hell yeah, he wanted this. "I just wanted this morning to be about you."

"I want it to be about both of us," she murmured before she took him fully into her mouth.

And his knees nearly buckled as she sucked him deep. Then he forgot to think, and at times breathe, as she worked him with her mouth, deeper and harder. Everything about her was magic, even in this.

"I'm about to come," he finally managed to rasp out, feeling completely out of control. He valued his ability to remain in control of himself at all times but now that Rebel's mouth was on him?

He didn't know his damn name.

She moaned around his length, not moving, so he let go of his barely there control, his entire body shaking as he came in her mouth.

He slammed his palm against the tile as his climax continued to hum through him, his knees weak and... hell.

He pulled her up from the hard tile and buried his face against her head as she did the same to his chest. He wanted to tell her that he loved her, but knew how it would sound if he blurted the words now, right after an intense orgasm. Not to mention she had her last show tonight. He wouldn't put any more pressure on her.

So he simply held her as he came down from his high and memorized every moment of this time together. When she allowed herself to be vulnerable with him in a way he knew that she never had with anyone else.

It was the same for him. Other than his friends, he'd never let his guard down with anyone, not truly. But it was even deeper with Rebel. She knew him on a fundamental level. Knew where he came from, had supported him long before he'd made something of himself.

The same was true vice versa. He'd always known she'd make it big. She had the star quality and raw talent that was rare. Now she was his.

As soon as tonight's concert was over, he was laying it on the line, telling her exactly how he felt.

# CHAPTER 21

"Why are there so many people back here?" Weston shouted into his radio. He had his arm around Rebel, with Juan and Nash on either side of them, as Nash ordered the random people backstage out of their way.

"Rebel, Rebel!" A young girl shouted for her attention but Weston held out an arm to keep everyone back.

There were way too many people here and he'd seen mob mentalities before. Situations like this were a powder keg and he wasn't letting it go off tonight. Nope.

Rebel's show had gone off without a hitch, the pyrotechnics even bigger than from the Friday show and the crowd had gone wild at her finale.

But as soon as she'd strode off the stage, however, shit had started to go haywire in the form of a mob of people. They'd been let in backstage during the last five minutes of the show, rushing past the guards with a rabid wildness. And he needed to get Rebel out of here *now*.

"They've all got backstage passes," Octavia, a Red Stone Security employee, said into the radio. "But there are too many of them. The general security let them through, but they shouldn't have. We're currently trying to guide most of them back out."

"I can sign some autographs," Rebel said above the din of noise.

"No," Weston growled, relief punching through him as they pushed into a mostly empty hallway. The noise started to dim as he and the other men guided her down the hallway back to her dressing room. This was utter insanity and someone's head was going to roll for letting it happen. He'd had strict protocols in place for letting people back here, had limited the number of backstage passes to a minimal amount and only people he'd personally vetted. "Stay behind me and start pushing them back," Weston ordered Nash and Juan.

Who both had mirrored expressions—frustration.

Something he was feeling too. This was bullshit. "There are too many people here," he told Rebel. "And I don't like the energy buzzing off the crowd."

"I don't either," she said quietly, tears forming in her eyes. "I didn't think we were having more people back here."

"We weren't supposed to." And he was going to kill whoever had given, or likely *sold*, a bunch of backstage passes. They'd been banning anyone who wasn't personally vetted for these last two shows, especially after what had happened on Friday night. Not to mention that Rebel had a *stalker*.

"Hey, stop pushing!" someone shouted from behind him.

"In here." Weston shoved open the dressing room she was sharing with Lia, saw the other woman packing up her things. "You two stay put. And lock the damn door," he added, before briefly kissing Rebel.

Then he turned and caught Juan, who a middle-aged brunette mom had just shoved right in his chest.

He snapped. "Hey!" He held up a hand, then whistled, hoping it would get everyone into some sort of semblance of order. It was like these people had lost their goddamn minds.

"We were told we'd get pictures!" a blonde woman who was older than him shouted, elbowing the woman who'd pushed Juan out of the way.

"Yeah, and autographs," the brunette shouted, with her daughter nodding along. When the blonde shoved her again, the brunette turned around fast and clocked the other woman right in the face.

God dammit. "No one goes inside," he said, pulling out his radio again as Nash and Juan strode forward and tried to calm the crowd.

The narrow hallway made it difficult for the people to rush, but this was a stampede waiting to happen and if it did, someone was going to get hurt.

"We need all backup in sector four. Now! Bring the police as well. Two women are engaged in a physical confrontation and—" He ducked as a pink sparkly heel flew past him, slammed into the dressing room door.

"I'm going to kill you, bitch!"

More shouts rose from behind the fighting women. He was glad Juan and Nash weren't getting in the middle of it. Their job was to keep Rebel safe from these nuts. The fans could have it out with each other for all he cared.

"Already on the way. Five minutes until we're at your location. We're coming in from the west side, but the police will be coming in from the south hallway," Octavia said, the radio crackling slightly. "I'm going to kill whoever let this many people in tonight!"

"10-4." He glanced behind him, saw that the hallway in the other direction was mostly empty but the tension in his gut didn't lessen. They better hurry the hell up.

***

"What's going on out there?" Lia asked as she continued folding some of her costumes and placing them neatly in her rolling suitcase.

Rebel was surprised the other woman was still here. Normally she didn't hang out after opening, even though Rebel had tried to befriend her. Lia was incredibly talented but didn't click with anyone on tour. Some people were just loners though. It sucked because it would have been really nice to have had a friend on tour. Someone who understood the ins and outs of everything, and how lonely fame could be. Her drummer and guitarists usually changed every year because of how tough touring could be, so while she'd always got to know the people she worked with, there weren't any deep bonds.

"No idea. A bunch of people have backstage passes and are acting like animals," she said, sitting down on the tufted pink couch, glad the tour was finally over—and looking forward to going home with Weston. Looking forward to a lot with him.

Their dressing rooms were much the same, though this one was slightly smaller. She laid her head back and just breathed evenly as she heard shouting outside. She wanted to open the door, check on Weston, but knew that wasn't a good idea.

"So are you dating him? The billionaire?"

"Ah..." Her instinct was to snap that he had a name, but she gave a neutral smile. "Yep. So what are your plans after this?"

"Not sure yet." Lia zipped up her suitcase and gave her a tight smile. Something about her expression was weird. "I've had a few offers to do shows out in Vegas, so I might."

"I'm sure Paige will be happy about that."

Lia just shrugged, then looked over at the door when there was a thud. "Jesus, it's no surprise that people who buy backstage passes for twenty bucks have absolutely no class," she muttered as she bent down to grab another bag.

Rebel snorted, but then paused as she digested the woman's words. "What did you say?"

Lia turned to look at her, her hand still in her bag. "What?" she asked, holding the bag close to her as she started walking in Rebel's direction, her sneakers quiet against the tile. Her eyes were dilated and there was something really off about her expression. She looked... almost manic.

Rebel stood up and took a step back, alarm bells going off in her head. "About the backstage passes?" Something was very, very wrong. How did Lia know someone had done that?

Lia was watching her too closely, her eyes too bright as she continued walking toward her. "You're such an asshole," she snarled, her mask completely falling away.

Rebel took another step back, running into the rolling cart of costumes, and tripped. She tried to right herself, but froze when she saw what had tripped her—someone's *leg*.

Wait, what? Oh my god! There was a man's too-still body hidden behind the row of clothes, but she could see a pool of blood now starting to form all around him.

"Yeah, I had to take care of that freak too soon." Lia made a tsking sound as Rebel stared down at the clearly dead man who'd been hidden by some clothes. "It's going to play out really well in the media—for me, anyway. He was hiding here waiting and attacked you, but luckily I was here and I killed him in self-defense," she said in a mocking tone. Then her expression turned gleeful as she continued. "Unfortunately you died from your wounds, and I'm going to be a hero." She laughed maniacally at that as she revealed her freakshow plan.

"Oh my god." This woman was nuts. She stepped over him, but slipped in blood and toppled over as full-blown fear slammed into her. "Weston!" she screamed.

"He's not gonna hear you." Lia shoved the rolling cart out of the way and jumping over the dead guy with ease—and that was when Rebel saw the glint of the blade in her hand.

No, no, no.

Rebel rolled over, scrambled to get away. She managed to shove to her feet, but couldn't move very fast on the tile with her bloody heels. She held up her hands as she stared at Lia in horror. "Look, we can talk—"

Lia lunged at her, slicing out with the long knife. On instinct, Rebel tried to block her.

Pain ricocheted through her as the knife sliced over her palm.

She screamed again, blindly reached behind her for anything and grabbed a bunch of scarves. Damn it! There was nothing here but clothes! She threw them at Lia as she tried to think of a way around the crazy woman with a knife. If she could just get the door open. But she had to get *to* the door first.

And Lia was directly in her way.

Lia's smile was unhinged as she shoved a vanity stool out of the way, still stalking toward her with the dripping-red blade.

Rebel's heart slammed in her ears. She slowly moved along the length of the long vanity, reaching behind her, trying to find anything to use as a weapon. Her fingers clasped around... a curling iron. She snatched it up and held it in front of her as she screamed again even louder. The insulation in these rooms was good but hopefully Weston would hear her.

She realized the curling iron wasn't on so she couldn't even use it to burn the other woman. Damn it!

There was a loud thud on the door. Then frantic banging.

"You're not going to get away with this." She took another step away from Lia, her heart about to pound out of her chest.

Lia just laughed and lunged again, her knife raised above her head.

Rebel kicked out, slamming the point of her high heel into Lia's thigh with all her might. Lia screamed, but slashed downward as she lunged at Rebel again.

Pain sliced through Rebel's forearm, but she ignored it and kicked out again, making contact with the woman's shin this time. As she did, she swung the curling iron wildly at her, but missed contact.

"Bitch!" Lia screamed but Rebel raced for the door, her heels slipping again as she tried to run. And she didn't have time to undo the straps on her blood-slicked shoes.

The door flew open suddenly, the frame completely busted. Weston stood there, face like a thundercloud as his gaze narrowed on them.

"She's crazy!" she screamed.

"Duck!"

Without thinking, Rebel hit the ground and Weston jumped over her. She was aware of Juan and Nash rushing in, but she turned toward the man she loved.

He easily ducked the knife slashing down in Lia's hand, grabbed her arm and—twisted it with an audible snap.

Lia screamed and the knife fell to the floor. Rebel dove for it, shoved it away with her hand even as Weston spun Lia, then flex-cuffed her hands behind her back.

Lia groaned in agony, but Rebel ignored her as two policeman and two more uniformed Red Stone Security people rushed in, weapons out.

"You're bleeding!" Weston was suddenly in front of her, his expression concerned.

"I'm fine," she said, feeling as if she was in a haze. As if everyone around her was moving in slow motion except Weston.

"You're not fine." He tugged his shirt off and wrapped her forearm tightly. "Damn it, this never should have happened," he growled to no one in particular.

The burning pain was just starting to register as the fear and shock faded. "She killed someone else. He's—"

Weston scooped her up while the police dealt with Lia. "We'll figure everything out later. I'm getting you out of here."

"There are already a couple ambulances at the east exit," Juan said, as he and Nash fell in around them.

Lights went off somewhere, and she heard gasps and so many voices as they spilled into the hallway.

She curled in on Weston, tucked her face into his neck as he shouted at people.

"Get the hell out of the way before I put my boot up your ass," he snarled at someone.

"Move it, move it!" Juan and Nash both shouted.

She closed her eyes even though she had her face buried against Weston's neck because she didn't want to look at anyone. Didn't want to deal with anything.

Lia had just tried to kill her. The reason didn't even matter. A woman she'd been touring with for most of the last year had tried to kill her, and had killed at least one other person. Oh my god, she'd likely been responsible for the stage accident. It made sense, considering she had access to everything and no one would question her presence.

"I'm sorry, sir, you're not allowed to come with us."

She opened her eyes and realized they were outside now by one of the main entrances, where half a dozen ambulances were lined up.

Weston's arms tightened around her. "I'm her fiancé and she's not going anywhere without me, so just do your damn job and stop the bleeding. Now!"

"He's coming with me," Rebel said, finally finding her voice.

The medic looked as if he wanted to argue, but nodded. "Come on then. Can you step up or do we need to pull the stretcher down?"

"No, I'm—"

Weston lifted her up so she could step into the back of the ambulance then jumped up behind her.

The EMT slammed the door shut behind them as his partner pulled away from the curb.

"She's got a knife wound on her forearm and one on her palm. The one on her arm is worse and is going to need stitches," Weston said.

"I'm going to need you to move back so I can look at her wound and start taking care of it." The medic's voice was calm as he gently nudged Weston out of the way.

"It's fine. I'm going to be okay," she added, more to calm Weston than herself. It could have been so much worse.

Weston frowned as he sat at the back and stared as the EMT started taking the T-shirt off.

As he did, she winced, and let her head fall back on the gurney. "That lunatic really got me good."

"You're definitely going to need stitches." The man's nametag read Stanley. "But a surgeon will make sure you don't scar." His voice was so calm and even as he began cleaning her wound.

She didn't care about scarring, but simply nodded and looked at Weston, trying not to wince as the EMT put antiseptic on her wound. But it was no use because it really stung. And that was when she felt more tears surging up, but not from the pain, so she closed her eyes.

They could have lost each other tonight.

Rebel wanted to reach for Weston, to hold his hand, but there was no room in the tight space.

She had so many questions about why and what had happened but the only thing she really cared about was Weston. He could have been killed by that woman. And if he hadn't gotten to her in time, she could have been killed.

So many scenarios bounced around in her head like a Ping-Pong ball.

"She's shaking." Weston's voice was tense, and when she heard a rustling sound, she saw he'd pulled out a Mylar blanket, the material crinkling as he ripped it free from the packaging.

"You can wrap it around her legs and bottom half, but stay out of the way." The EMT continued to work, was now asking her about potential allergies, but all she could focus on was Weston as she answered the questions.

Before she knew it, they were pulling up to the ER.

Weston must have read her mind, because he moved in and held her hand as the doors flew open and the EMTs moved into action.

"I want to leave," Rebel grumbled. She'd been at the hospital all night and now most of Monday and was ready to get home. She'd already changed into the clothes Anna had dropped off and wouldn't be staying here one more night.

"Soon." Weston was at the foot of her bed, not looking at her as he furiously texted someone.

"What's wrong?" she murmured. "I mean other than me being in the hospital and a woman I worked with trying to kill me."

He shoved his phone in his pocket and slid into the bed next to her. She was in a private room and they hadn't balked at her security, not that it would have mattered. Nash and Juan were outside her door and not going anywhere until their backup arrived. At least according to Weston, because he and Paige had been handling everything. She'd mostly slept.

But now she was cranky, her arm ached from the eight stitches and she hated the way the painkillers made her feel. All loopy and out of it. Ugh.

"Nothing to worry about."

"Come on," she murmured, cuddling up to him. "You've been in an even worse mood the last hour. And that's saying something."

"I've been the picture of calm."

She snort-laughed. "I can't tell if you really believe that." She looked up at him incredulously, her hand gently draped on his chest.

He shrugged, which told her that yeah, he might actually believe it.

"You threatened my doctor."

"He was moving too slow and your second one is a lot better. She actually knows what she's doing."

Yeah, her first doctor had been kind of pompous but she hadn't cared. Weston sure had though, and he'd made sure everyone knew.

There was a knock on the door, then Juan popped his head in. "Detective Duarte is here."

"He can come in." Rebel started to sit up, but Weston simply grabbed the bed controller and raised it so she didn't have to.

"Hey, you look great," Duarte said. "The news made it sound a lot worse."

"They don't know shit," Weston growled.

The detective just snorted as he stepped farther into the room. "Are you okay to talk?"

"I'm good," she said before Weston could respond for her. "I would have talked earlier but I figured you were just busy handling everything. But I have a whole lot of questions."

"Ah." He flicked a glance at Weston. "We were told you weren't up to talking to anyone."

Rebel just sighed but didn't respond to that. "Well I'm good now. So... what the heck happened? Why did she try to kill me? Has she talked? What about the dead guy?" After Lia's little villain speech, she had sort of an idea, but not fully.

"She's got a lawyer now and is trying to plead mental insanity but I don't think it'll stick. Not with how premeditated everything she did was. From what we've gathered so far, she lured Ed Reeves into believing that she was your agent or assistant and convinced him that you wanted to meet him."

"Wait, the guy stalking me? The one who sent the gross messages?" She looked at Weston. "Did you know any of this?"

"I knew he'd been the one killed. But I didn't want you to worry about anything."

Oh, they were going to talk later about him keeping her in the dark, but not in front of an audience. "Okay, so she told me that she had to kill him 'too soon'."

The detective nodded. "That lines up with what we've learned so far. She lured him with the intention of making it look like he killed you, and then she planned to kill him afterward and play the hero. But according to her, he got too handsy with her and she was forced to kill him. Claims it was self-defense. Right now we're not sure what's true and what's not. She hates you, Ms. Martinez. Truly hates you a terrifying amount. She was ranting about how much you didn't deserve anything, some pretty nasty stuff." He shook his head, disgust on his face. "She wanted to headline her own tour and about a month ago was told that wouldn't be happening anytime soon. It sounds like that's what pushed her over the edge into violence."

"What about the rush of people backstage? What the heck happened? Lia couldn't have sold all those passes by herself."

"She sold them to someone on one of those anonymous online places, told them to sell them for twenty bucks a pop right near the end of the concert. As far as we can tell, the buyer wasn't involved in anything else. Just someone dumb enough to get involved in her scheme. And her ex-boyfriend is the one who hacked the cameras and corrupted some of the security feeds on Friday and Saturday. Apparently some of the software wasn't fully updated, and they used it to hack into the system. But the ex is talking freely in exchange for a reduced sentence. Said he had no idea that Lia planned to kill you. He was still hung up on her and she used that to her advantage."

"You believe them?" Weston asked, his tone hard.

"I do." The detective gave a slight nod. "Her ex is in real shock right now. I think it's why he's being so forthcoming with us. And even though I know what happened, I'm going to need an official statement from you, just for the record," he said, looking at Rebel. "But after that, I don't think I'll need anything from you for a while. The state's attorney might end up reaching out if Lia wants to take this to court. But my instinct tells me she won't. The court of public opinion is already shredding her to pieces."

"They are?" Weston hadn't turned on the news, or let her turn it on. He'd insisted she needed rest and no outside distractions. And while he wasn't wrong, she was going stir-crazy.

He nodded, his expression grim.

By the time she finished giving her statement, Paige strode into her room, her expression unlike anything Rebel had ever seen. She looked pale and almost drawn. She nodded politely at the detective as she approached the bed.

"Rebel, I'm so sorry about Lia. I had no idea that she was—"

"You don't have anything to be sorry about."

"Well, she was my client too. God, I... I just..." She shook her head, seemed to clear it a little. "It's a big shock. But I wanted to let you know that your label is bending over backwards right now to make sure that you're happy. I think because she was on their label too, they're worried about getting sued. But who knows. You can take a break for as long as you want."

The truth was, Rebel hadn't thought of the future past getting home, healing up and adopting her new dogs. And... what she wanted with Weston. But work hadn't really crossed her mind. "Thank you. I'm honestly just ready to get home."

Paige nodded. "Of course. I've got a car service all lined up and Anna has handled everything else. Apparently Lia had been making nasty threats to her, telling her that you were planning to fire her. Turned her into a nervous mess. She'd been looking for other work because of it but now that she knows what kind of person Lia is..." Paige shook her head.

"Once Weston gives me my cell phone back, I'll reach out and thank her for everything." She shot Weston a frustrated look.

"You haven't been online the last thirteen or so hours then?" Paige looked surprised.

"No."

Paige shot a sly look at Weston, then looked back at Rebel. "Your boyfriend here has been all over the news. That shot of him carrying you out of the concert without a shirt on has been on twenty-four seven. I've even been contacted by some producers who think you'd make a great action hero. God, that jawline," she said, shaking her head.

Weston looked at Paige in horror.

Which made Rebel laugh. "You were on the news?"

"All. Over. It." Paige sighed and picked up her purse. "It's a shame you already have a job you love because Hollywood would also love that jawline."

Weston just snorted but didn't respond. Which was pretty standard for him.

"And," she said as she headed for the doorway, "since I know you're never going to tell her, I'm doing it myself."

"Paige!" Weston's tone was hard as he slid out of the bed.

She lifted an unapologetic shoulder as she looked at Rebel. "Weston paid for that influx of marketing a couple years ago. The one you thought the label paid for. It was him, and he made me promise not to tell you. His company had just gone public and he decided to invest in you because, and I quote, 'She's the most talented person I know and deserves everything she's ever wanted.' Be mad all you want, Weston, she should know how much you care."

Paige left before he could respond, the door easing shut behind her.

Rebel turned to stare at the man she loved. "You paid for all that marketing? For real?"

He shrugged, shoved his hands in his pockets. "I had way more money than I knew what to do with and you were a good bet."

"Oh, is that it?" She swung her legs off the bed and stood, ignored the twinge of pain in her arm and palm. It actually made sense why Paige hadn't seemed to get frustrated with him just taking over her security the last week. "I was a good bet?"

"What do you want me to say? I've believed in you for as long as I can remember but I knew you wouldn't take the money. So I had to be sneaky about it and I'm not sorry." His ice-blue eyes were defiant as he stared down at her.

"I love you, Weston Davis. Not because of the money, but because of who you are. You are the kindest, most giving person I've ever met, and I'm never going to *not* love you. So unless you decide to leave, you're stuck with me forever." Saying the words out loud made her feel more vulnerable than she'd ever felt in her life. But if she couldn't be real with the man who'd seen her at her worst, the man who'd literally saved her life, then what was the point?

He moved so fast she barely tracked him as he wrapped his arms around her. "I love you too. I didn't want to say it and scare you off."

"Scare me?" Her laugh was slightly manic. "My life is a nightmare. That woman could have stabbed you," she said on a cry, stupid tears stinging her eyes. "I'm terrified you're going to realize that I'm not worth all the bullshit that comes with me and—"

He crushed his mouth to hers even as he gently embraced her. His kiss was a hard claiming, no other way to describe it. When he finally pulled back, he was breathing hard. "You're worth everything, Rebel. I've been in love with you since I was fifteen and I almost told you so many times. But I never wanted to get in the way of your dreams."

Tears rolled down her face as she clung tight to him. "*You* are my dream, Weston. My family." Her everything.

He pulled her to him again and she buried her face against his chest. The only thing that mattered right now was Weston and this moment.

# CHAPTER 23

*One week later*

"Oh my god, turn that off," Weston groaned as he stepped into the living room and saw what Rebel, Anthony, Bailey, Elliana and Van were all watching.

It was a replay of him carrying Rebel out of the concert and yelling at people to get out of his way. And she couldn't stop watching him in action. Paige was right, he really did look like a superhero.

"No way!" Rebel gently scratched behind Jupiter's ears as he lounged on her lap. She'd picked up him and Lucky on Friday just as she'd planned. They'd been skittish at first, and not ready to check out her entire house, but as of this morning, they'd both been super curious and had decided to venture into different rooms and into the entire backyard instead of just the little fenced-in area off the pool. Jupiter had gone a little crazy chasing squirrels and tired himself out.

Lucky was currently being carried by Weston—who she was absolutely obsessed with, something Rebel could appreciate. The yippy little Chihuahua loved Weston almost as much as she loved Jupiter. She liked Rebel just fine, but Rebel had a feeling it was going to take longer for them to bond. But that was okay, she wasn't going anywhere.

She pressed play, grinning as the image of Weston carrying her out of the stadium moved across the screen. She chose the slow-motion option so he looked like he was part of an actual action movie or something. The first time she'd watched the video, which was now viral, it had been shocking to see. Especially since she'd still been trying to process that her coworker had tried to kill her out of stupid jealousy.

Apparently Lia had been livid that Rebel got such a huge marketing push, deeming it 'not fair' since she'd been with the label longer than Rebel. And the longer she'd toured with Rebel, the more her hatred had festered. Then being rejected for her own tour had pushed her off the deep end. At least she was in jail now and never getting out.

Grumbling under his breath, Weston sat on the couch next to Rebel. "I'm getting so much shit about this at work."

Elliana cackled. "It's hilarious. Even some of the guys from our old unit have been reaching out asking if he'll sign autographs for them." She tossed a piece of popcorn into her mouth, then said, "Not that I don't enjoy watching Captain America here, but can we turn the movie back on? I want to see the real Cap doing his thing."

"Fiiiine." Rebel turned the movie back on as Jupiter turned around to nuzzle Lucky. And to Rebel's surprise, Lucky jumped in her lap, circled a few times before she found a comfortable spot and curled up. "You better not pee on me again," she whispered.

Lucky looked up at her as if to say "no promises" but nudged her hand until she gave her pets. Then Rebel laid her head on Weston's shoulder, leaning into him as she mostly ignored the movie.

She didn't care about the movie at all, but she loved this sense of normalcy with her friends.

*Friends.*

It had been an eternity since she'd felt normal and she'd wondered if she'd ever have something real like this. Now she knew. And she couldn't believe she'd ever been jealous of Elliana. I mean, okay, the woman was gorgeous, but she was so funny and kind and never looked at Weston the way Rebel looked at him. And apparently she had some weird thing going on with her neighbor that she'd promised to tell Rebel about later.

Soon Anthony would be heading off on tour, but they'd been friends for years and she knew that distance wasn't going to change anything.

At the sound of the doorbell, Lucky jumped up and dashed away, barking her little head off. Jupiter didn't bark, but followed after her best friend, tail wagging.

"That's gotta be Molly, Tag and their kids," she said as she stood. The security at the main gate had a list of people they let in the neighborhood and she'd given Molly the code to her gate.

The others ignored her and Weston as they hurried after the dogs.

"Or Juan and Angel," Weston said.

"I didn't think they could make it." She stretched her arm out slightly, was counting down until she could get her stitches out. At this point it was just itchy more than anything and she was grateful there hadn't been any nerve damage.

"They had a change of plans. He texted me, I forgot to tell you."

"Oh good." She was looking forward to meeting Angel in person. It looked as if Nash and Juan were going to be her bodyguards whenever she needed them and for East Coast concerts. Rodrigo was still healing and while he was good at his job, she'd meshed so much better with Juan and Nash.

Through the glass doors, she was able to see that it was not only Molly and family waiting, but Juan and Angel too. The kids were jumping up and down, already in their bathing suits, which made her smile as she opened the door.

"Hey!" Molly hugged her before greeting the two pups.

"Pool is that way," she said, pointing for the kids' benefit. "Go crazy."

They screamed in delight and took off running.

Tag just snickered as he followed after them, murmuring, "You're going to regret that comment later."

Jupiter dashed off with the kids, but Lucky was jumping on Weston, demanding to be picked up. She was small, so of course she wanted to be carried and in the thick of things.

"She's our little diva," Rebel murmured as she shut the door behind everyone.

"I'm going to follow my little demons to make sure Tag's alright," Molly said as she hurried in the direction of her family.

"Rebel, Weston, this is my angel, Angel." Juan had his arm around a petite brunette with stunning curves and a wide smile.

"Thank you so much for inviting us into your home, especially after all you've been through."

"Oh, I'm fine. Or mostly fine. No swimming for a bit, but other than that I'm great. And if you brought some of those amazing pastries, I might invite you back without Juan."

Angel grinned and lifted up a cloth bag that looked to be filled with a couple boxes.

"Okay bestie, follow me then." As they headed back toward the kitchen and pool, Rebel had to fight back a sudden, unexpected push of tears.

Her entire life she'd wanted a real family, to belong. To have people she could call when she needed. And now she could actually believe that it might happen, that her circle could grow wider if she'd let people in. She slid her arm around Weston as they entered the kitchen to find Elliana making a plate of just chips and candy.

Most of the kids were in the pool already with Jupiter, screaming and having a good time with their dad, while Molly sat at the island top eating her food in peace.

To her surprise, Anthony raced out of the living room and headed for the pool, cannonballing like a kid himself.

"And he hasn't had any wine," Bailey murmured, joining them in the kitchen with an adoring smile on his face as he watched his boyfriend through the wide panel of windows.

"How are you feeling?" Weston murmured as he kissed the top of her head, his voice low enough for only her as the others got settled and started making plates of food.

"Really good." She kissed his cheek and smiled up at him. "And in case I haven't told you today, I'm glad you're mine."

He got that wild possessive look on his face that she loved as he brushed his lips over hers. "I never get tired of hearing it."

***

Weston watched Rebel as she flopped onto her bed next to him. "I'm so tired," she said into the pillow. Then she rolled over and winced as she adjusted her injured arm. "I don't understand how Molly and Tag deal with all their kids. And they're so good with them, so patient." She laid back on her pillow, shaking her head slightly.

Everyone had left an hour ago and while he'd cleaned up, she'd taken the dogs out and showered. And now had on only her little robe and clearly no panties. Which he was trying not to notice since he'd been holding off on sex the last week.

"How do you feel about kids?" he asked, reaching out and cupping her cheek gently.

"Um, I like them, but I don't want any right now. Maybe in like five or seven years? What about you?"

"Same," he said around a grin. And after seeing Molly and Tag's kids today, seven sounded about right. "Oh, Lizzy texted again to say that she wasn't missing the next get-together."

"I can't wait to meet her in person."

"She said the same about you." One of Lizzy's kids had had a soccer tournament or some kind of sports event so the family had been out of town all day. But he had a feeling that Rebel and Lizzy were going to get along when they finally met. Even Lizzy's maiden name was the same as Rebel's last name.

Jupiter raced into the room, dove onto the bed and flopped down next to Rebel. Lucky wasn't far behind, though she had to use the little steps they'd bought for her to join them.

"You're glad everyone is gone, huh?" Rebel murmured as she cuddled Jupiter close, nuzzling his head.

Jupiter just licked her face, then shut his eyes. Both he and Lucky had run off about two hours into the party and hung out in Rebel's room. Then they'd come out a couple hours later, played some more, then left to get some quiet. Her place was certainly large enough to allow them space when they needed it.

"I don't know why we bought them beds," she said on a laugh, scritching under Lucky's jaw.

"Because I'm about to get you naked very soon and they're not going to be hanging out in bed while we do it. Unless you're too tired?"

She sat up, her eyes gleaming. "I'm not the one who's been holding out all week."

"You've been healing." He nudged the dogs toward the end of the bed and maybe they understood because they didn't whine at all, just headed for the big round bed they shared by the window.

"Not my vagina," she practically pouted.

He let out a burst of laughter. "I was trying to be thoughtful."

"I don't want thoughtful. I want orgasms." She was definitely pouting now.

"God, I love you," he growled as he pulled her on top of him. Even though he wanted to pin her beneath him, with her arm he wanted to make sure he didn't accidentally injure her.

"I love you too," she murmured against his mouth. "And... I'm just curious if you've moved in here. Because a bunch of your clothes are in my closet now."

He watched her carefully. Apparently he wasn't as slick as he'd thought. "Is that a problem?"

"Nope. I was going to ask you to anyway. Or we can move into your place."

"Let's just start calling them our places and we'll figure the details out later," he said as he slid her robe off her shoulders.

"I like that idea. Ours." She hitched in a breath as he cupped her breasts, rolled his thumbs over her hardening nipples.

Soon he was going to make it official, put a ring on her finger for the entire world to see. Very soon. The entertainment feeds were already speculating about them and while Rebel hadn't said much publicly since her attack, she'd posted that single picture of her kissing him with a simple heart as the caption. That was it. But it was enough to make people go bonkers with theories of how long they'd been together and a hundred other things.

He didn't care what the world thought, just her. But that caveman part of him wanted the world to know she was off limits for the rest of time, so he loved that she'd publicly made a statement without saying a word at all.

He was hers.

# EPILOGUE

*Six months later*

Weston brushed his mouth over Rebel's, wishing that he could deepen it, but that wasn't what tonight was about. "Why do you seem so nervous?" he murmured, sliding his arm around her as they walked up the steps to the raised concert area at the Miami Beach Bandshell.

The space was unique in that it was completely open overhead, but had a wall surrounding the venue so that it had that outdoor feel while still being private-ish. It was a beautiful, clear night and even though it was summer, the constant ocean breeze and fans were keeping the place cool.

They'd reserved the place for an exclusive auction mixed with performances from various Miami musical artists. All the proceeds from the evening would be split between three different organizations. Molly's pet shelter, a local community center that did a lot of after-school programs, and a women's shelter that had been a safe haven for decades. They'd wanted to give back to their community specifically, to the city they'd grown up in and that had always loved them. Rebel had been working on this auction for months and now that it was finally here, everything was going off without a hitch so far.

Normally the Bandshell could accommodate over thirteen hundred for a regular concert, but since it was catered, they'd had to cap it at five hundred.

All the wealthy people of Miami had been vying for tickets. It was wild how fast the tickets had been snapped up. But that was the thing about exclusivity and the chance to see a concert like this, with select artists. He knew that about half the people here probably didn't care about who they were giving money to, but in the end, as long as they gave, that was all he cared about. Thankfully Rebel and Weston had reserved some tickets for their friends ahead of time.

She leaned into him, pressing her body up against his as they reached the outer wings of the concert area. The last performer was wrapping up and Rebel would be going on stage in the next few minutes. "So many of our friends are here. People I really like," she murmured, looking down at the giant emerald ring on her left-hand ring finger. "It's different performing for friends than strangers, I guess."

He kissed the top of her head, so grateful they were together and that soon they'd be getting married. He felt as if he'd been waiting for this moment for most of his life. "Some of them have seen you do a terrible winner's dance when you beat everyone at Pictionary. And they've seen you play water volleyball. I don't think you need to worry about anything."

She snickered and buried her face in his chest for a moment. Then she looked up at him, her expression full of love. "You really did an incredible job picking this out." She held out her hand, looked at it for the hundredth time in the last few days.

"Well, I had a little help. Emphasis on *little*." Weston had known a diamond was out; Rebel didn't like them. Emerald was the natural choice of gem since it had always been her favorite, but he'd brought Anthony with him because the man had impeccable taste. And because he'd wanted Rebel to have exactly what she wanted. After months of research, he'd ended up having something custom made—because Rebel was one of a kind. The brilliant emerald-cut emerald was surrounded with a halo of round and baguette diamonds, making it sparkle under *any* light.

An ocean breeze kicked up then, the salt-tinged air and string lights crisscrossing the concert area the perfect backdrop for the evening. North Beach was only steps away from them, and after this he was going to ask Rebel if she wanted to go on a moonlit walk along the beach before they headed home.

Home. Where he lived with her.

"I hope everyone is ready for our next performance!" Bailey was the announcer for the evening, as he'd been helping Rebel with this project for months as well. He'd completely leaned into his roll of auction host and was killing it. Weston was pretty sure that Bailey and Anthony would be getting married next.

"Knock 'em dead," Weston said, kissing her again as she strode onto the stage.

Rebel wore a short emerald-green dress and high heels, her grin wide and infectious as she strode onto the stage, waving at everyone before she took the mic from Bailey. "Thank you all for being here tonight!"

Applause and whoops went up from the crowd, making her smile more.

Out of instinct, he scanned the area but they had this place locked down tight. And ever since all the bullshit with her stalker and Lia, they hadn't had any real problems. Sure there were assholes online who loved to leave nasty comments about Rebel, but he was learning to ignore it like she did. They were creating a life together and at the end of the day, he didn't give a shit what strangers thought about anything.

"I have a couple surprises for you tonight! The first is a surprise auction *just* for you guys. I've never done anything like this before but thankfully Bailey has organized everything so..." She paused, her smile growing, and to his surprise the entire crowd quieted, hanging on her every word.

She was amazing.

"I'm offering up a private concert to whoever gives the most to one of the charities here tonight. You get a great tax write-off and a party! It can be for an anniversary, birthday party or a random Tuesday. Bailey has all the details at one of the tents at the back, so I hope you all give big to one or all of these incredible places we're here tonight to support. And I've also decided to do a raffle concert to everyone else who gives."

A cheer went up and she laughed, the sound like music as she continued talking.

"You guys did a really good thing," Paige murmured, as she slid up to stand next to him.

"Thanks. This is mostly Rebel's doing."

Paige just snorted softly. "Just take the praise, Weston. You're worse than her," she murmured, no heat in her voice. "And I know neither of you did this for the publicity but it's generating so much more than I think even Rebel imagined. Certainly more than I did. The online auctions were a great addition for people who couldn't be here."

"*That* was my idea," he said, smiling as Rebel continued talking to the crowd about all the good they were doing. The last six months his job duties had slightly shifted and he loved it. He was still a partner in his company but they'd brought on more people who were doing a lot more hands-on stuff. Which had been the original goal in the first place; to get it built up into something big so that they could step back and hire people to do the day-to-day.

It had given him the time to learn more about Rebel's business—and spend more time with her, which was pretty much his life's goal anyway.

And ironically, when she'd pulled back and put her next tour on hold, a handful of television execs had reached out to Paige about Rebel being a judge on a musical competition show.

"Do you know if she's going to take the job?" Paige asked.

He knew exactly which one she was referring to, but he just lifted a shoulder. Rebel was going to take it since the show was based in Miami. It was like a dream come true for her. She could finally deepen her roots here, and if and when she decided to tour again, they'd figure things out then. He didn't tell Paige only because it wasn't his place to do so.

"You're mean," she grumbled.

He shrugged again, but couldn't hide his smile as Rebel got her game face on. She was about to start and she hadn't let him hear what she'd been practicing. It was the only secret she'd been keeping from him the last few months, and now he finally got to hear what she'd been working on.

"This is my last surprise of the night. Probably." She smiled as a few people chuckled, but continued. "I have a new song I'm going to perform tonight. It's dropping to all the streaming services at midnight but you're hearing it first. This song holds a special place in my heart. I wrote the first version when I was seventeen and in love with a boy who is now my fiancé. He doesn't like the spotlight but just for tonight, I'm sharing a little bit of our story. For years our jobs kept us physically separated but we were always in contact."

Clearing her throat, she looked right at Weston, her eyes filled with love. "He's the best friend I've ever had and this song is for the seventeen-year-old boy who stole my heart, and now for the man who's shown me what it's like to be loved unconditionally. I don't know if the words will do our love justice, but I'm going to try."

He forgot to breathe as her words rolled over him and then as she started singing, he saw no one and nothing but her. As she sang about young love turning into something deeper and loving the one person who's seen her for who she truly is, his throat tightened with emotions.

She was telling the story of them, and he felt it all the way to his marrow.

Some days he questioned himself about waiting to make his move, about if he should have said something earlier, but as her beautiful voice wrapped around him, he realized that it didn't matter. Because they had each other now. They'd figured things out and were now creating a real life together. If his aunt could see them, he knew she'd be smiling.

As the song ended, the crowd erupted into wild applause, their claps and shouts vibrating against the stone around them. He wasn't even aware of moving until he was in front of her and pulling her into his arms.

"You like it?" she asked against his neck, her words barely audible above the noise surrounding them.

"I love every single word you just sang," he rasped out.

"So it was worth me keeping it from you?" She pulled back to look up at him.

In response, he crushed his mouth to hers, claiming her for himself, for her, for the whole damn world to see.

She'd just laid herself bare, told the entire world what he meant to her, and he wasn't sure there was a better gift than that. The only thing he knew was that he was going to spend his whole life continuing to show her how much he loved and treasured her.

# Dear Readers

Thank you for reading Protecting Rebel! If you'd like to stay in touch and be the first to learn about new releases you can:

1. Check out my website for book news:
   https://www.katiereus.com
2. Follow me on Bookbub:
   https://www.bookbub.com/profile/katie-reus
3. Follow me on TikTok:
   https://www.tiktok.com/@katiereusauthor

Also, please consider leaving a review at one of your favorite online retailers. It's a great way to help other readers discover new books and I appreciate all reviews.

Happy reading,
Katie

# ACKNOWLEDGMENTS

I owe a big thanks to Kaylea Cross for her help getting this book into shape. And I'm also grateful for my editor Kelli Collins and proofreader Book Nook Nuts (Tammy) for helping me put the final touches on this. For Jaycee, I'm thankful for another great cover! To Sarah, do you ever get tired of my thanks? Because I'm brimming with it! Thank you for all the things. And even though this isn't technically book related, I'm so grateful to my mom (who will never read this book, lol) for all the ways she helps out. Because of her I'm able to write more than I would otherwise. And of course I'm thankful to all my readers! You all are the ones who wanted more, more, more of this Red Stone Security world and I will forever be grateful.

# ABOUT THE AUTHOR

Katie Reus is the *New York Times* and *USA Today* bestselling author of the Endgame trilogy, the Ancients Rising series and the MacArthur Family series. She fell in love with romance at a young age thanks to books she pilfered from her mom's stash. Years later she loves reading romance almost as much as she loves writing it.

However, she didn't always know she wanted to be a writer. After changing majors many times, she finally graduated summa cum laude with a degree in psychology. Not long after that she discovered a new love. Writing. She now spends her days writing paranormal romance and sexy romantic suspense.

# COMPLETE BOOKLIST

***Ancients Rising***

Ancient Protector

Ancient Enemy

Ancient Enforcer

Ancient Vendetta

Ancient Retribution

Ancient Vengeance

Ancient Sentinel

Ancient Warrior

Ancient Guardian

***Darkness Series***

Darkness Awakened

Taste of Darkness

Beyond the Darkness

Hunted by Darkness

Into the Darkness

Saved by Darkness

Guardian of Darkness

Sentinel of Darkness

A Very Dragon Christmas
Darkness Rising

**Deadly Ops Series**
Targeted
Bound to Danger
Chasing Danger
Shattered Duty
Edge of Danger
A Covert Affair

**Endgame Trilogy**
Bishop's Knight
Bishop's Queen
Bishop's Endgame

**Holiday With a Hitman Series**
How the Hitman Stole Christmas

**MacArthur Family Series**
Falling for Irish
Unintended Target
Saving Sienna

**Moon Shifter Series**
Alpha Instinct
Lover's Instinct
Primal Possession
Mating Instinct
His Untamed Desire
Avenger's Heat

Danger Rising

Protecting Rebel

**Redemption Harbor® Series**

Resurrection

Savage Rising

Dangerous Witness

Innocent Target

Hunting Danger

Covert Games

Chasing Vengeance

**Redemption Harbor® Security**

Fighting for Hailey

Fighting for Reese

Fighting for Adalyn

**Sin City Series (the Serafina)**

First Surrender

Sensual Surrender

Sweetest Surrender

Dangerous Surrender

Deadly Surrender

**Verona Bay Series**

Dark Memento

Deadly Past

Silent Protector

**Linked books**

Retribution

Tempting Danger

***Non-series Romantic Suspense***
Running From the Past
Dangerous Secrets
Killer Secrets
Deadly Obsession
Danger in Paradise
His Secret Past


***Paranormal Romance***
Destined Mate
Protector's Mate
A Jaguar's Kiss
Tempting the Jaguar
Enemy Mine
Heart of the Jaguar